P9-CAJ-162

bunny **MODERN**

also by david bowman
Let the Dog Drive

a novel

david
BOWMAN

bunny
MODERN

LITTLE, BROWN AND COMPANY

Boston New York Toronto London

this novel is for Dr. Spock,
Dr. Seuss, &
Jonathan Lethem, M.D.

Copyright © 1998 by David Bowman

All rights reserved. No part of this book may be reproduced in any form or by any electronic or mechanical means, including information storage and retrieval systems, without permission in writing from the publisher, except by a reviewer who may quote brief passages in a review.

First Edition

The characters and events in this book are fictitious. Any similarity to real persons, living or dead, is coincidental and not intended by the author.

The author is grateful for permission to include the following previously copyrighted material:

Excerpts from "Glow Worm" by Johnny Mercer, Paul Lincke, Lilla C. Robinson. Copyright © 1952 by Edward B. Marks Music Company. Copyright renewed. Reprinted by permission of Edward B. Marks Music Company.

Library of Congress Cataloging-in-Publication Data

Bowman, David.
    Bunny modern / David Bowman. — 1st ed.
        p.   cm.
    ISBN 0-316-10281-4
    I. Title.
PS3552.08757B86   1998
813'.54 — dc21   *97-25429*

10 9 8 7 6 5 4 3 2 1

MV-NY

Text design by JoAnn Yandle

Published simultaneously in Canada by Little, Brown & Company (Canada) Limited

Printed in the United States of America

contents

1 narcotic spaghetti western   1

2 big pink cone heart   23

3 radio city overdose   64

4 ballad of a thin man   81

5 modern bump and grind   107

6 animal magnetism   124

7 tales from the reagan era   136

8 postmodern   160

9 astaire as metaphor   201

"You have a child . . . watch out."

—Dorothy Kalins
"New Parents' Style: Bunny Modern"
New York Times, October 21, 1993

bunny **MODERN**

1 narcotic spaghetti western

YOUNG WOMEN, let me address you directly. I bet your names are either Emily, Alice, or Ishmael. How do I know? Because my father named you. Yes! Imagine those days before the Millennial Blackout, when your parents were just youngsters rehearsing your conception. In those days wattage buzzed above the avenues. A man's home was so wired that electricity poured from spouts in the walls. Extension cords snaked under every carpet. And oh, the glow! Televisions and laptops and surveillance monitors illuminated the night.

And lightbulbs! Let me tell you about lightbulbs — I hunger for those knobs of hollowed glass as if they were illuminated fruit. The nights were so alive back then that I bet your father reached up from the couch and *killed* the lights so he could grope your mother with only the glow of the TV to guide him.

Those were the days when my father — fashion guru supreme — had his first vision of Lit Wear. His subsequent devotion to the publication of hems and stitches and spaghetti straps was tireless, but not even he foresaw that his Nineteenth Century Lit Couture would make Lewis Carroll, Saint Emily, even Herman Melville, as big as Elvis.

At this point most of you Alices and Emilys shake your curls and say, "Your father had nothing to do with my naming." You'll claim that the name Alice predates Charles Lutwidge Dodgson. Emily comes years before "My life had stood a loaded gun." Okay. Technically you're right. Both names are even older than AC/DC — Ben Franklin surely flew his kite above the wet heads of many Emilys and Alices.

But Ishmaels — forget it.

If my dad had not stitched your fathers' Melville trousers and your mothers' Melville blouses, you would all be strangers to your call. You were born into an America without electricity. But imagine an America with no Lit Wear. Your caretaker would have leaned over the rail of your crib and called out something conventional, like "Good morning, Baby Chelsea!"

But thanks to Lit Wear, your parents feminized a Biblical name that was never in vogue to begin with, and christened you Ishmael. That's why I favor you more than those Emilys and Alices who deny that my father named them.

As for my name — I hate it: Dylan.

Say it — *Dylan*.

Dyl pickle.

That name can be denied my father as well. My mother chose it. (Kiss me and taste the vinegar on my lips!) My father wanted Nathaniel, but Mom shook her head. "Too GOP."

So instead of being Nat, I ended up Dylan. Me and a hundred thousand other men. And a few women. All named by our mothers back in the last decades of the Twentieth Century — a time of kilowatts and power lines.

I know the retro-Marxists among you are shaking your hot heads. You believe we still live in a time of kilowatts — the power companies secretly shooting volts into the sockets of the rich. Why else would the windows of the mansions in Beverly Hills and Grosse Pointe be lined with blackout curtains? The rich hide their light.

Sounds good on paper, but I believe Con Ed. I've sat through a dozen public lectures about how some "Morphemic/Quantitative Aberration" triggered the electrons in AC/DC to begin speeding in their orbits. Run faster and faster until they were spinning faster than light. Perhaps faster than time itself.

I've heard all the theories: Con Ed's electric current has volted itself into the past and the ancient Greeks are paying power bills now. Or maybe Nefertiti. Or if electricity is like karma, it only flowed back a century to Thomas Edison in Menlo Park. . . .

Well, I say let Tom keep his volts. The days of wattage weren't so great. I'm old enough, Ishmaels, to remember wires and sockets, when Manhattan's Great White Way referred to the glow of theater marquees instead of big shot Caucasians. I remember how fathers wandered the streets strapped to their Walkmans; how moms knelt at the household TV, channel-hopping through network product.

My own mother did the network kneel, but my dad never did the Walkman walk. He ignored VCRs. *Miami Vice.* All of it. Instead, he began his first sketches of Lit Wear in the Reagan days and twenty years later looked up from his deathbed to watch his boyfriends modeling the new line of Melville couture — those young blond men in their Omoo pants and their Pequod shoes and their Billy Budd shirts. I tell you that my father died smiling like a baby. America was about to become literate again!

• • •

Let me follow in Dad's footsteps and sew a few words. Write you a first-person wardrobe in the present tense. God writes this way, although I'm influenced by memories of Mom's TV more than the Bible. Not that I'm the star of the show. My protagonist is female.

A George Eliot kind of fem.

A Brontë-style girl.

She is a little older than you, but young enough I can get away with using the G-word *girl*. God knows (speaking of G-words), my protagonist is a dozen years younger than me — she was just a kid when electricity became history. But there's nothing juvenile about this tomato now. The first time I see her I do a double take. *Wow!* I say to myself. Then I'm puzzled. *What's so exciting?* She's dressed a little funny — wearing a pair of slim Jane Eyres under a Bret Harte duster. That sounds like a mismatch, I know. But it works.

Her name is Clare. She'll tell me her father chose it from one of Hawthorne's posthumously published romances about a little Puritan girl buried alive in an avalanche. Although — as I said earlier — there's nothing girlish about Clare, she fits Puritan intentions. She is a severe, askew beauty.

Picture her almond-shaped cheeks with their almost Mongolian contours. It will sound crazy, but I see Clare's face as being from some past electric era paradoxically more modern than our own. Say, the 1920s. Old photos reveal that women then were streamlined curves of chrome with their tight dresses and cropped hair. They were modern in a way that no modern girl has been since.

Not that Clare is ever adorned with Art Deco nose-pegs. She never wears earrings. No rings or lipstick. The first time I see this woman her only accoutrement is a baby — she's strolling through

Washington Square in Greenwich Village holding a child. The imp looks bored, flicking its fingers in front of its face. *What are these little things. Oh. My fingers. I've seen these before.* A little mirrored reflector is stitched on the baby's bonnet. The kid looks like an old-fashioned surgeon.

I know Clare is not the mother.

It's in the air.

I bet some of you are Isis fanatics who believe only women have psychic powers. I'm a guy who follows Rupert Sheldrake's Twentieth Century guidebooks. You know, the ones postulating that human thoughts and memories and even intentions resonate across the atmosphere as signals called Morphic Resonance. When electricity vanished, we discovered he was right. Some men found they could forecast the weather, while many women began taking dictation from the dead. I can sheldrake too. I'm one of those guys who pick up the experiences and stories and memories of others in his head — although my ability is gender-specific: I can only sheldrake women.

Don't think this dismisses the mystery of your gender. Female Morphic Resonance is never simple or obvious. For example, I can sheldrake Clare's nonmaternal state but don't realize that she's a nanny until the gunplay starts — an understandable oversight perhaps, because Clare is not wearing her guns in the open like other nannies do.

Are any of you carrying a piece? Your *life stood a loaded gun?* Modern girls know a hundred ways to hide their magnums under a pretty Jane Eyre. But nannies always hang their pistols around their hips like cowboys.

To discourage kidnappers.

I appreciate that there are no guns around her belly immediately. I'll later learn she keeps her heater tucked under her arm because she hates holsters flapping her flanks. Another man may smell his girl's nylons and smile, but I will grow to crave the fragrance of Clare's single holster — especially when the leather is moist and earthy.

Don't hold Clare's nanny status against her. When you were a kid, there wasn't an epidemic of white-collar Americans out kidnapping babies. In those early Blackout days, children were still being born. Every hour. Every minute. There were so many tykes to go around that your caretaker tormented you for sport. Not anymore. What's the frequency nowadays — two births a day in Manhattan? Three for the tunnel-and-bridge crowd? Both Columbia Presbyterian and Con Ed claim the birth rate plummeted because of men, not women. Men, and, of course, the absence of volts. Doctors tell us that semen is just a form of slow electric current without the charge, each sperm sympathetically aligning itself with a corresponding electron. They theorize that if electrons are orbiting backward, a man's tadpoles must swim backward too. Away from the womb. Away from the egg. *"Let's get out of here, boys!"*

My own doc believes that the only reason that a few babies are still being born at all is because of a biological counteroffensive: The mothers' eggs became predatory. Hunters. Your baby brother is here because some hungry egg got lucky.

Of course, there's no proof that this is true. It's not like anyone can attach a movie camera to an electron microscope and find out what's going on down under. I'll let other writers speculate about sperm on the run. But we all know nannies are armed because kidnapping has become rampant. Grannies kidnap fully grown children. Milkmen climb through windows to snatch newborns. When I first see Clare and her baby, she is heading toward the nanny corner of the square — "Niagara Bawls." Aptly nicknamed, as you can hear the squall of crying babies all through the park.

How do nannies ever get used to the din? In Manhattan, biological parents stay as far away from the nannies as possible. In Washington Square, real parents sit with their babies at the eastern edge of the park, within the confines of a safety pen strung with bright Easter egg barbed wire — Real Mom and Real Dad jiggling their young under manned gun turrets.

Tourists ask, "Why keep the nannies out?" I'll tell why: Local ordinances require nannies not only to remain indifferent to the babies in their care, but also to encourage the kids to holler and cry. This assures the parents that the nanny and baby aren't bonding, because — God forbid — then the nanny might kidnap the child herself. In the Op-Ed page last Sunday in the *Times,* yet another antinanny Californian squawked that "an East Coast nanny up-bringing is a deterrent to healthy childhood development." Oh, blah, blah, blah. The citizens of the Golden Bear are just jealous because they can't afford armed nannies themselves.

Most New Yorkers have the bucks for nannies, as well as illegal narcotics — which is what the economy of Washington Square Park is all about. Dudes and dudettes slouch every ten feet selling designer drugs and reefer. Clare's path takes her past two who appear to be selling joints 'n' bags.

I say "appear to." As dope dealers, these kidnappers can act nervous "naturally." See the chick say to the guy, "Cops." The dude quickly drops to a crouch, as if he is hiding a Baggie of weed in his shoes. But Clare ducks too — kneeling eye-level with the guy, baby in one arm and the other extended holding a gun, an action that causes the baby to begin shaking its arms, laughing.

"Shut up, rat," Clare says, with gritted teeth. She says this to the baby, not to the man kneeling before her black pistol — a compact semiautomatic made of plastic, of all things, ridiculously called a Glock.

Regardless of the dumb name, the gun looks lethal. It gets the guy's attention. And this encounter is not lost on the nannies at Niagara Bawls, where the eight women stand as one — each nanny suddenly holding a handgun, save for a squat one who whips out a sawed-off shotgun from inside her baby buggy.

You know that nannies are usually hard women, but if you could see this crew! Do any of you smoke? You wouldn't think twice about striking a match across any of their cheeks. And get what they're wearing. The two nannies gripping magnums sport Ambrose Bierce boots and Devil's Dictionary burnooses with the hoods down.

Ah, Nannies from Hell.

The ones with Colt .45s are all fitted in Poe. There's a few pairs of Marie Rogêts. A Ligeia sweater. One woman even wears a tight Masque of the Red Death skirt. The only nanny not wearing Lit Wear is a beanpole girl with a bushel of black hair above her ears. But with that sharp nose — her beak — she might as well be bleating, "*Nevermore. Nevermore.*"

The Poe vibe stops with the other faces. One nanny has a classic George Washington pinched jaw. Another is more toothache and nosebleed. The most cheerful nanny is walleyed, her forehead ringed with green aboriginal tattoos.

Wait. I finally register that the nanny with a harelip is wearing Lit Wear *von Kraut* — her body sheathed in a soiled Critique of Pure Reason jumpsuit.

Each of these nannies is just standing there, doing nothing. Just waiting. Watching to see if Clare needs backup. While the man who is eye-to-eye with Clare's Glock is saying, "It's cool. It's cool."

He drops the crowbar that he had slipped from his pants and holds his palms out empty. Clare is supposed to think that he was intending to hit her knees. Steal her baby. But something seems wrong. What are these amateurs really after?

His female partner's face is tense, but tense with excitement. I sheldrake her thoughts — *Things are going as planned.*

The guy on his knees sees that the nannies are all distracted. He almost smiles. Then doesn't. He doesn't want to give anything away. I'm the only one besides him who sees the plump woman hurrying between the chess tables at Niagara Bawls. Sees the woman dip down into a beige baby carriage. Whip up holding the child. Then this babynapper abruptly leaps over a cement park bench and lands on the sidewalk in a small cluster of pedestrians. Suddenly the plump woman becomes two — both women instantly running in opposite directions. Both holding babies. One is a decoy. But which one? Then a cart blocks the intersection. Suddenly a third fat woman appears running with a baby. She's heading west toward Sixth Avenue.

The nannies have been taken in by a plot originally conceived by Louisa Alcott in an unpublished story that was discovered by a professor of literature at NYU. He's kept the story secret all these years so he can sell the plot to customers he hears are sniffing around the black market baby trade. Today's buyer is a senior editor at Calvin Klein. The fake dope dealers are juniors (junior editors, that is). At this very moment, the editor is standing on top of a hot dog cart at the eastern edge of the park, watching the scene with what looks like a pirate's telescope. (Actually, it's the device his wife uses to peer at birds in Central Park.) The bird-watcher herself paces below the cart, asking, "How is it going? How is it going?"

"So far, so good," the man says, so breathlessly that his wife can barely hear him.

Now two of the nannies — George Washington and Raven Beak — are rapidly pushing the baby buggies into a circle while the plump one with the shotgun jumps atop a chess table. She peers down at a dozen New York University types who have gath-ered on the sidewalk, all with the same hungry look on their faces — *Unattended babies. Unattended babies.*

"Stay away, dog-fucks," the fat one spits, poking her sawed-off in the air as her compatriots begin to sprint down MacDougal. Five armed nannies chase the wagon rolling downtown. They know which woman had the real kid. The nannies only hold their fire because they don't want to hit the baby. After the cart blocked the view, each nanny knew that all of the runners became de-coys — the real child is now hidden on the cart. The nanny with the forehead tattoos shouts, "Shoot the ponies, girls!"

Man! I have to tell you that the resulting gunfire is just *pop! pop! pop!* MacDougal Street has history, but it has nothing to do with gunplay. My namesake used to live here. In the days before I was born, Bob Dylan rode his motorcycle from one sidewalk café to another until he ended up at Kettle of Fish. Anyway, once the nannies start firing, no one cares about folk history. The horses rear and bolt across the concrete, the cart bumping over the cobble-stones.

The Immanuel Kant nanny stands behind the others, aiming her gun my way. I see her features clearly. And wish I didn't. This woman's harelip makes her face appear sideways. The Colt goes off. The chubby decoy running east goes down. The harelip nanny spins and fires at the decoy running north. That decoy is hit too. The woman takes it in her shoulder. Crashes through the doorway of a store — no, the doorway of a Christian Science Reading Room.

The harelip starts laughing. Many nannies are, in fact, Christian Scientists. I sheldrake that the harelip certainly isn't. (Neither is Clare, for that matter.) But the boss of this particular nanny company is. The harelip knows that to finish the decoy babynapper off in a reading room will be sublime pleasure in the fullest Immanuel Kant sense of the word — *sublime* equaling *beautiful violence,* e.g., an eagle fighting a snake in the air.

This particular prey is now inside the reading room, crouched behind a bookcase clutching her shoulder, whimpering. Rocking back and forth. Let's say that this woman is a proofreader by trade. Her name is Constance. She thought a little bit of babynapping would be more exciting than inspecting paragraphs and hems. But Constance never figured on getting shot. When the bullet first hit, her shoulder and collar felt as if they were suddenly part of an apparatus much bigger than her body. A monstrous scaffolding. Invisible, and towering as high as the steeple at St. Patrick's. As she assimilated this vision, she stumbled into the reading room, thinking, *Thank God. Sanctuary.*

Big mistake. We all know a reading room is not a church.

The harelip nanny walks through the doors singing. Her song sounds like an old Beatles melody with simple new lyrics composed of just two words, "Fresh meat. Fresh meat."

It's a song about the drug she's on.

There's no reason — no practical reason — for this nanny to pursue the decoy babynapper in the reading room except for the sublime pleasure of it. Some grotesque sport. She's peaking. It's the drug that nannies are on. Not even Seattle's retired grunge junkies dare to play around with nanny dope. Most of us can't even imagine being a nanny *au naturel,* let alone one who is tripping. I went out with a nanny once or twice a few years ago when I lived in Park Slope, and she told me they take drugs because of Nannies' Paradox: Nannies are conditioned not to bond with the baby they're caring for, yet they're also trained to lay down their life for the child if they have to. How can a girl reconcile these two states?

Vengeance.

Nannies sniff lines of Vengeance — although in a jam they use a hypo too, which is why they have tracks on their ankles. I myself do occasional hits of youth drugs like Twenty Something, and my chemist tells me that Vengeance works like this: When adrenaline hits a nanny's brain, she is instantly filled with mother-animal instinct. The nanny will do everything possible to protect her baby until the adrenaline has subsided — presumably because the kidnapping has been prevented and/or the kidnapped child recovered. But a nanny can't be allowed to feel any joy. Nor can she be allowed to think too much about Nannies' Paradox: *I was willing to throw down my life for a baby that, frankly, I don't give a shit about.*

So come with me into a nanny brain when this drug twists

and gives her a different endorphin. A different high. Suddenly the vengeance switch is flicked on. Most nannies agree that this part of the trip possesses audibility, sounding like a bass drum beating the words, *Vengeance. Vengeance. Vengeance.* This is why nannies always kill the kidnappers, then shoot up the bodies.

And the harelip nanny finds her *fresh meat* hiding behind Bengal translations of *Science and Health.* Constance looks up. Eyes wide with fear. With her good arm she holds up the plastic baby — the goo-goo ga-ga decoy. "See? It's not even real."

"This is," the nanny says, raising her gun and holding her free hand over her mouth. This nanny, named Katrinka, will not allow a babynapper to be terrified of her harelip. Her lips are God's private joke on her.

"What's your name?" Katrinka asks.

"Why do you want to know," the injured woman answers.

"I want to know what your name is before I shoot you."

Constance gasps, then shouts, "Shoot me? You're not going to shoot me."

"Yes I am," the nanny says, moving her hand closer to her mouth. "What's your name?"

Constance winces. *My shoulder — it hurts.* "I won't tell you," she replies. "I won't tell you."

The nanny sighs. She lowers her free hand, then makes a puppet mouth with her fingers.

"All right then," her hand says. "Say cheese."

Katrinka answers in a different voice. "All right, Ms. Hand — *cheese.*"

She smiles her harelip at Constance.

Talk about twisted.

Talk about sublime.

The cornerstone of Mary Baker Eddy and Christian Science is mind-over-matter. Mind-over-disease. But what nanny's brain is big enough to overcome that particular pair of lips?

The smiling nanny fires four times. Three shots are Vengeance. The fourth is for God.

Clare is one nanny who is opposed to the cerebral architecture of Vengeance. She'll later tell me she prefers to peak with the rescue of the baby and tries for premature vengeance state whenever possible. Let's go back in time a few minutes. Clare is still on her knees as her fellow nannies start shooting at the carriage with a wad of Vengeance in her cheek like chewing tobacco.

"Stand up," she barks to the kneeling man.

He gets up. "Careful, sweetheart. Be cool."

"What's your name?" she asks.

"Edward Mars," he whispers.

"Take care of Mr. Mars," Clare says to his partner. She quickly turns sideways to protect her baby from any blood spray and shoots Eddie Mars in the stomach. Then Clare leaps up and heads toward Washington Square South.

She sees everything. She knows the woman running in her direction isn't a decoy. That woman has the real baby. The other nannies were fooled by the babynapper's body language — but Clare isn't. The babynapper doesn't run like a woman gripping a doll. She runs like a man cradling the real thing. She is a he, a babynapper wearing drag. When he is shot by the harelip, only

Clare sees him roll over and kneel — the kidnapped baby still in his arms — then shake his head. Stagger up. And continue running.

Police vest.

Clare stops and raises her Glock. But the baby that she is holding reaches too. Giggling. Bouncing its head, causing the little reflector on its brow to produce visual pops of glare and sun spots. Clare extends her arm. Aims for the babynapper's head. Easy shot. And with his brain gone, his shoulders and elbows will lock, and he'll stay gripping the baby in his arms.

Monique thinks differently. That's the name of the baby in Clare's arms. This nanny will describe Monique as a tolerable baby. She will say this the way you'd say, "My head hurts, but it's tolerable." But now, the child starts bawling — giving out twisted *whahs*. The volume of the complaint louses up Clare's shot and she shoots out the window of a church.

The nanny stares down at the child and says with gritted teeth, "Shut up, runt."

Clare took night school courses to perfect this look. The philosophy of the class is a belief that everything that will happen to us is already recorded in our brain. Including our own death. The look Clare gives the baby makes the kid see that same vision.

If it doesn't, no matter.

The child immediately shuts up. You may ask, "Why on earth should the kid continue living now that she's seen her own Inner Death manifested in the world?"

Valid question.

But it's not my concern.

By sheldraking, I only function here like some floating camera. What I'm seeing right now is Clare looking away from the baby and sighting down the barrel of her gun. She pulls the trigger.

Clare loves her Glock because "there's no hammer bite to distract a girl." She shoots the running man exactly where she is aiming — his skull taking the XTP Jacket Hollow Point bullet in the rear, JFK style.

Clare now starts running herself, Baby Monique in her arms. The man continues for two more steps, then he stumbles to his knees on the street.

But now another man is at the body. The editor. When Clare is perhaps twenty feet away, his wife steps out from the hot dog cart with her rifle. "Stop. I don't want to hurt your baby," she calls.

Clare stops.

"I'll fire if I have to," the wife says.

Clare lowers her Glock. And says, "Shit."

"Turn around," the wife orders.

Clare does. At this movement, the editor exhales. The baby he's holding begins pawing at his nose because his nose is a shiny thing. This baby is named, of all things, Dylan (please tell me that this name is passé beyond belief in your region of America too). I'll hear later that this new father — this false pirate father — is a Whitman freak who intends to name this child Calamus. And don't think *re*name. The pirate father doesn't even know the name of the baby in his hands. His choice will be this child's true name. "Forget your old name, this will be your only relevant christening," he says to this baby, then intones, "'For you these from me, O Democracy.'" He laughs. "'To serve you *mon homme!*'"

Clare doesn't hear his words, but their force apparently resonates *Walt Whitman, Walt Whitman,* because Clare whispers, "I celebrate myself . . ." and peers into the reflector on Monique's forehead. And in ironic glory of our wattless era, Clare begins reciting "I Sing the Body Electric": "Upper-arm, armpit, elbow-socket, lower-arm, arm sinews . . . and Glock." She recites these words raising her gun hand above her own head, as she simultaneously kneels, arches backward, and then shoots the editor's wife.

An upside-down shot.

Glorious shooting. Oh, the glorious backbone of that nanny! What choreography!

And I'll tell what I withheld from you. The editor's wife was about to shoot Clare in the back. The wife was thinking, *Why not two children?* She was licking her lips over the baby in Clare's arms. *A little Ishmael for me!*

I could have told you this earlier while Clare's back was still turned. But then you would have thought Clare fired in self-defense. She didn't. She was going to kill that woman regardless. And the editor's wife takes Clare's bullet in the chest. The woman is blown backward. Her husband starts shaking his head back and forth, his consciousness oscillating from glory to mystification (*What's going on? Where did that nanny get her gun?*) to absolute horror (*This is my wife. That was my beloved. We married before the electricity disappeared*).

He opens his mouth and takes a step toward her body and starts talking. He tells his wife the plots to her favorite Harding novels. He tells her about what he is editing now. They both used to talk lots — over wine, over coffee. They were each other's favorite companions. They'd yack for hours about fashion and literature. They'd discuss things of substance: Their needs. Their Inside Child. Their desire for a whole-grain diet. Their craving for a son. And now his wife, his Electric Age bride, is lying there, a hole in her chest actually exhaling breath.

He takes another step.

"No," Clare shouts, pointing the Glock. "Give me the baby."

He looks at the child. So quickly his. So quickly gone. He reaches out his arms and hands the child to her. Clare cradles the new kid in her gun arm. Like dogs checking each other out, the two babies, Monique and Dylan, reach and coo at each other.

Clare turns and walks with the babies away from the editor.

The other nannies run up and Clare tells them, "We have a stable situation here, girls."

Raven Beak and George Washington exchange looks. The one with the tattoos says, "Vengeance." Then the nannies all start chanting, "Vengeance. Vengeance."

All except Clare.

"Let him be," she tells her sisters. "He already wants to be dead."

The nannies all nod, but continue walking to the editor and his wife.

"He'll eat the gun someday, don't worry," Clare calls over her shoulder. Dylan starts squirming furiously, and she glares at him. She doesn't have to say anything. That baby stops and begins trembling — a hot-wired neurological response that shouldn't have kicked in until the child was at least two or three.

It takes all day for Clare's dose of Vengeance to wear down. Although I don't actually follow her, sheldraking makes me like God and Santa Claus: I know everything that happens. I know that Clare considers going to the movies — there is a Valentino playing at St. Marks. But St. Marks is a crummy crank-joint. Their lanterns are dim. You stand there cranking the nickelodeon, squinting at the silent movie through an eyehole crusted over with God knows what. People who are addicted to watching flicks at St. Marks all wear Coke-bottle glasses.

Instead Clare goes home to her fifth floor walk-up on East Eighth and Avenue A. This is unexpected: no tech-nostalgia inside, the space mostly wood and brick, with no shrines to television or telephones. Just a candle burning beneath a portrait of Gaston Glock. She must really be into pre-tech comfort, because above the cast-iron potbellied stove hangs a reproduction of *American Gothic*. Wait a minute. Gaston Glock isn't Clare's household saint. There's another *American Gothic* in the hall, hanging above Clare's static electricity treadmill. Let's slap our foreheads! This woman has a reproduction of *American Gothic* in every room. How can a girl be this sober? And we know she has a thing about pistols, not pitchforks . . .

Clare is in her bedroom now, where she lines up five pairs of shoes on the floor, not a high heel or flat among them. No retro-Manolo Blahniks or even modern Jane Austen slingbacks. They're shoes for men — all ten of them.

God. It would take forever to tell you the psychological reasons for this state, including her father's taste for Japanese papershoes, but whatever the reasons, for the past five years Clare has actively collected the footwear of her "paramours." But she only takes traditional nonliterary shoes like oxfords or wingtips. She'll never swipe a pair of Tom Sawyers. This nanny got the oxfords she's holding now the morning she started fighting with

Paramour #1 and he stomped out of her apartment wearing her flip-flops. He never came back. The same story with Paramour #2 — except he left loafers. Clare can't remember how she acquired Paramour #3's wingtips, but she stole #4's the morning that she realized there was going to be a #5. The shoes of #5 were a surprise. She took these brogans on impulse. Then, that night, the man was sitting shivah at his father's house and a chandelier fell on his head. No more #5. She waits for #6.

After I sheldrake the death of #5, my own forehead starts hurting. I'm up in my apartment on West Forty-seventh Street. My mammal-radio goes dead and I'm no longer receiving Clare's history. Instead, I'm hallucinating a static silhouette of a horse galloping. Big stallion. Galloping frame-by-frame like a Muybridge photograph. He's mounted by a shrouded rider — see the outline of sickle resting on rider's shoulder. The black horse and rider move across my sight lines left to right, then back again. Each time, moving closer. I've seen this vision a few times before now. His identity is pretty obvious. Forget what you've read about a "pale horse." The Thanatos stallion is black black black. But I've never seen the rider so close before. I can actually make out his profile. I'm a child of the Technicolor age, so the Reaper looks like Clint Eastwood to me. Eastwood is a cowboy like Tom Mix except starker. More John Barrymore.

And this particular vision is why guys who sheldrake can be real drags — we're susceptible to visions of death. My big questions now are: Why in conjunction with Clare? Who is slated to die, me or her? Eventually we both will die, of course, but does this horseman mean the end is soon? If so, is it preventable? And finally, am I sheldraking death, or is death attached to sheldraking?

I stand up and light all the lanterns in my bachelor crib. I don't want any shadows anywhere. I dump a shovel of Blue Coal into my stove and brew up some joe. I nurse my mug and this conviction comes to me. If I don't see Clare again — in the flesh or in a sheldrake — I'm the one who'll die. That sounds ridiculous to you, I know. You probably figure that the Reaper only rides in reaction to the gunplay at Washington Square Park and my mysterious horseman is a nanny thing, not a sheldraking thing. Well, I hope you're right and I'm wrong. And speaking of death, let's back up. What of the nannies and the editor? Did the Reaper ride over him? You assumed the worst, I know. But let me show you what happened: The editor knelt at his wife's body. Talking to her of fashion. Listing his favorite authors. Probably thinking of how much his wife loved fashion and literature and children. How much they missed electricity . . .

The walleyed nanny with the forehead tattoos walked over and leaned into his face. "Whadda you do for a living, buddy?"

He looked up from his wife. "I'm an editor at Calvin Klein."

"What were you gonna name the baby?"

"Calamus," he answered.

"That baby's name is Dylan," the nanny told him. Then she looked the editor in the eye. Unlike Harelip's deformity, her eyes have nothing to do with God. And she has never had any qualms about using her deformity as vengeance. She raised the hood of her Devil's Dictionary and fired. Not at the editor, but at his wife's body. Again and again. And I'm telling you about this because although it seems cruel — this is Manhattan.

Forget vengeance and justice — they're philosophical states

found only in pharmaceuticals. The editor was stealing a baby that belonged to another man and woman. What of those parents' loss if he had succeeded? Did the editor consider that? No. He's due compassion, but certainly not sympathy.

I stand on the side of the nannies. The tattooed one shoved her magnum in her belt, then bent down and wiped the wife's blood off her husband's slack jaw, whispering, "Publish or perish."

Then she walked away.

2 big pink cone heart

BAD WEEK, Ishmaels. All I do is have visions of that damn Black
Rider, so I go cold turkey on sheldraking. Then on the seventh
day, I see Clare again. By accident! Not in the park, but in New
Jersey, of all places — and no, neither of us is here to make one
of those Menlo Park *Oh-God-give-us-back-our-watts* pilgrimages.
I'm here casing out a house. Not that I'm a cat burglar or real
estate broker, just know there are people inside that house that
can make me big money. Most of Jersey is owned by the Japanese,
and this neighborhood is full of prayer wheels and kites and bill-
boards written in Mishima-ese. In the middle of a neighborhood
of quasi pagodas, there is a pink house — a simple two-story, two-
family residence. Built in old-fashioned New Jersey colonial. The
house's color is delicately faded like an antique valentine, not gar-
ish like Dylan's old Big Pink in Woodstock.

I'm standing several houses down, casing out this Jersey Pink.
Suddenly a cop trots by on his palomino. I don't really look like
I belong here, so the cop slows to a lope, giving me the eye. I just

smile and crack my wrists. He keeps on going. When I look back at the pink house, Clare is standing on the porch in her Jane Eyres, sniffing a compact of Vengeance.

Oh, that delicate nose! I instantly feel better than I have all week. To hell with the Reaper.

But what's this nanny doing in Jersey?

There are two doors on the porch, one for the downstairs and the other for a second-floor apartment. A sign saying JERSEY BOUNCE STUDIO hangs over the downstairs door. That's the one she raps. A beat later, an old man appears, squinting through his reading glasses. "Yes?" he says.

Surely this man is familiar to Clare. Although she has never seen him in the flesh before, she has all those pictures of *American Gothic* up in her apartment, and now standing before her is a dead ringer for that old guy with the pitchfork. Clare is tongue-tied for a moment, wondering if he's a relative.

Then, she speaks — and I'm not sure how much of her dialogue I'm actually overhearing and how much I'm sheldraking. But she tells him, "I'm Clare from the Nanny Broker Company." She pauses. "I'm here for the Lindys."

Mr. Gothic relaxes. "Good. Hi. I'm Lindy."

She is relieved. There are no Lindys in her family. I'll tell you what Clare's thought means in a moment, but right now Lindy is leading her inside the house, saying, "My wife is out with the baby. Let me show you around."

The man doesn't ask to inspect her gun. That's odd. Clare thinks so too. She steps into a foyer that leads to an alcove. I can see her head turn. She glances left — a dim hall. Turns right — a living room. Then she looks down at Lindy's feet just as she feels the first rush of the Vengeance, and blows her whole serious worker routine. Clare is crouching and saying, "Beautiful! Beautiful!" Ah.

His shoes. It figures. They're pale, with no laces, classier than moccasins. The suede is padded, fat, and each shoe is bleached immaculate, with no scuffs on the toe or backquarter.

Clare realizes that she is kneeling at the man's feet and quickly stands, saying, "Wonderful shoes." She's out of breath.

Lindy smiles and says, "Thank you." Mr. Gothic is bemused.

"What in the world are they?"

"Fencing shoes."

She crouches again. "Do you mind?"

"It depends on what you want to do." He is still smiling.

She gives a laugh. "Shouldn't you be wearing one of those masks?"

"Masks?"

She stands and jabs her right arm up and out — swordplay. He gets it. "Oh, no. I don't fence. I teach dancing." He points at the sign on the door. "I'm Jersey Bounce." He does a quick shuffle-ball-chain. "These shoes are just the best."

He then waves his hand. "Come with me."

Now I'm with them in my mind. Sheldraking. I see everything: Clare pauses. She suddenly views this house with a nanny's junkie eyes: Living room — sunken floor of slippery wood. *The shitty little tot could slip and break a limb . . . or neck,* Clare thinks.

Metal end tables with sharp edges. *Poke out an eyeball. Cyclops kid!*

Kerosene lamps. *Burn the little sucker up.*

Dog Model gramophone on the floor with a dangerous crank. Clare imagines the needle cutting into a baby as it spins on the turntable, like side one of *Blonde on Blonde* made out of flesh and tissue. She's thinking these things now, but once she meets the baby, she'll pluck out her own eyes before she'll let anything happen to that *stinking filthy baby*.

Lindy is the cat that I want to eventually meet, but I'm so relieved to see Clare again, I can't proceed on my mission. I can only stand on this curb sheldraking this beautiful woman. Clare follows the man. They pass a wooden pedestal that holds the household shrine — in this case, a small rectangular box the size of a Chinese slipper carton. It's made of black plastic. There is a small hole in its side, ringed with chrome. The electrical cord is coiled into a mandala, where a candle sits. What's this dinky box anyway? I bet you and your family have a shrine to something big. A pot of incense smokes on a television or a washer-dryer. Clare doesn't recognize the Lindy shrine. Then, as they walk, someone starts clumping above their heads in the apartment upstairs. Is it a child? No, the gait is strange. A dwarf?

"One man's ceiling is another man's floor," Lindy sings, as the upstairs footsteps now sync with Clare's and his. Then the old man points over his shoulder. "It's an electric pencil sharpener," he says.

She gives him a blank look.

"The shrine."

"Oh," she says.

"The nursery is this way . . ."

The old man leads her down a back hall lined with bookcases full of modern lit — Calvin Klein first editions. Clare glances for copies of the books her father wrote. Each has his photo on the French seam along the spine. Nope, none.

Mr. Lindy leads her past a door, saying, "Bathroom." Another, "Bedroom." One more, "My wife's office." Then he says, "Me and my wife chose a pencil sharpener because it was the most indulgent electrical device we could think of." He laughs. "The neighbors all worship electronic necessities, but we choose to honor electricity's nonchalance." The old guy does a brief skip with his feet, then suddenly says, "Nursery . . . ," his voice inappropriately edgy as he points at a final room at the end of the hall.

Clare sticks her head into a room that justifies his tone. The space is empty of everything but a crib and a changing table. The crib is baby blue, the headboard marked by a sleeping bunny. The table resembles an ironing board despite the cartoon bunnies leaping across the rubber mat. Clare notes that this looks like a good surface for snorting lines of Vengeance.

The walls of the nursery are bare, with the old outlets painted over. The carpet is gray. Next to the door is a small platform, more wedge than shelf, where the safety lantern sits. Ah, the predictable decal — a bunny in a miner's helmet.

That's it. No other furniture. No miscellaneous baby doodads. A single gray nipple lying in the corner. Clare stoops and picks it up.

"Soda's," Mr. Lindy says, pointing at the crib.

That's the baby's name?

"Soda as in soda cracker?" Clare asks.

"No," he says. "You know the Soda Mountains in the Mojave Desert?"

"In California?"

"Yes."

"No, Mr. Lindy. I've never been west."

"Oh."

She waits for him to complete the thought — to say something like, "Well, my wife and I named our baby after those mountains because . . ."

But he doesn't. Nothing. Well, it's not like Clare is going to bond with this baby, so she lets it go.

Lindy glances out the window and asks, "Did Kathleen explain the arrangements?"

Clare pauses, then answers, "No."

He whips his head to her. Big frown.

"We were supposed to meet," she says. "But Ms. Keegan's schedule crashed."

My instant thought: *Keegan. Kathleen Keegan. I know that name.*

Clare's thoughts (instant and otherwise): *What's the big deal?* You see, nannies are routinely rotated out of each household after six months, and Clare was at the end of her shift with Baby Monique in Greenwich Village. *How complicated can a New Jersey baby be?*

Mr. Lindy's thoughts: *Buzz-buzz . . .*

The man is unhappy, but Clare has trouble reading him (and I can't, of course). His frown seems a dose of maximum Gothic. Give this harsh guy a pitchfork now . . . Know that Clare is not like those thousand other girls gone on *American Gothic* just because they crave post-tech comfort. She is obsessed because of lineage. She's related to the man who posed for the painting. That's why she wondered if she and Lindy were kin. Second cousins or something. Don't forget, the subjects of renowned paintings were once alive. Whistler's mother is someone's grandmother's grandmother. De Kooning's women nest in dozens of family trees. Mr. Gothic — in reality not a farmer with a pitchfork, but a dentist from Dubuque — left progeny too. Clare's father was his youngest son.

Clare has never seen a face like Mr. Gothic's — Mr. Pitch-fork's — in the flesh before. It's not sexy, exactly. She just had the sudden urge to run her fingers along the line of his Puritan jaw.

She finds herself raising her hand again —

Then someone begins rapping at Lindy's front door, so Clare follows Lindy back through the house, posed to pull out her gun. She relaxes when Lindy lets in a middle-aged Asian couple. Clare knows they're Japanese, not Vietnamese or Beijing Reds. Both visitors have granny glasses and berets and are wearing flip-flops. The man is holding two small black cases that look like high society pocketbooks. One by one — the man leading — they give quick bows. *Ah, Japanese for sure,* she thinks. *Doing those fake bows for us barbarians.*

"I'll be with you in a moment, Mr. and Mrs. Samora," Mr. Lindy says, letting them out a side door. A moment later, Clare sees the Samoras pass by a back window, doing their machine trot across a space more courtyard than backyard. Clare moves closer to the window and sees the two pause at the door of a small building. A garage? The man hands the woman a black case, and she then slips out a pair of killer stiletto high heels with toes so black they look wet.

Oh, to see the man's shoes, his floorburners!

The nanny presses her forehead against the window, but the Japanese man hurries inside the building without changing shoes. *Damn!* Clare spies a polished floor and a grand piano before the door shuts.

Suddenly the nanny feels breath on her neck and whirls, reaching for her gun. But then she sees the baby. And starts to gag. As the child scowls and thrusts tiny fists forward, Clare sees that the baby is held by an old woman.

"Oh, hello, dear," Mr. Lindy calls from the end of the hallway. "We didn't hear you come in."

How did you sneak up on me? Clare wonders, noting the old woman's faded I Could Not Stop for Death winter coat. What's that peculiar small pouch hanging around her neck? It's not some Lit Wear pendant.

"Good, you're finally here," the woman says, shoving the child directly into the nanny's face.

Clare scrunches her nose and takes the little body. It's a typical seventeen-pounder. Smells like a baby. It's got a baby brow. A baby fist. The nanny pinches the baby's butt — pinches hard, but the child doesn't cry. The baby just paws at her nose. Clare starts sweating. This is the most unnerving baby she has ever held. But why? She has no idea. She just feels like she's a girl again, with her stepmother nagging, "Clare, stop playing air guitar. Little girls play air baby." Not that there's anything imaginary about this baby. Clare starts doing a cake-from-the-oven maneuver (you know the pose: The nanny holds the baby outward with stiff indifference — as if the child were a loaf of hot angel food). Then the nanny finds herself unsure of her grip. What's this about? Clare has never done a baby-drop — not even in training when she ran the obstacle course with a doll in one hand and a semiautomatic in the other, shooting at targets — paintings of kidnappers — as they popped out of the ground.

A drop of sweat rolls down Clare's forehead, while Mrs. Lindy just stands there with a superior smile. *This woman is testing me.*

Mr. Lindy breaks the silence: "Why don't you two get acquainted, dear. I have to send a bird."

Dad walks down the hallway to a large black birdcage by the kitchen. Clare frowns — the cage door is not childproof. Then the baby begins squirming in her arms, kinetic energy that makes it hard for Clare to keep her grip.

Stop your wiggling, little shit-twit, Clare thinks.

What gender is it? Who cares. Babies are babies. Babies are beyond gender. The child now arches back and sucks in a breath. The air goes still. Then the baby emits a howl. *At last!* The kid's howl twists into a persistent yammer and Clare gets technical, tries to identify the crying. It's not a cry of discomfort from Clare's pinch. This mouth is not screaming for food. The diaper feels dry. She gives a quick peek. Empty. This is no typical tantrum. There is pride at the root of this cyclone of *whah* — the triumphant sound of something holy.

"The baby hates me," Clare says with pride to Mrs. Lindy.

The old mother just leans against the front door and nods. That's a surprise. Gray-moms aren't usually so calm, it's like she's been through the drill before. When Clare teaches classes for novice nannies, she lectures, "Postmenopausal mothers are the worst clients of all. Basket cases of anxiety. They keep the shades drawn in the nursery and insist you place a gun on every table. At the same time, they remember Spock child-rearing. It bugs them to the core of their being when a nanny forces their baby to cry. They usually plead, *You don't have to pinch the baby anymore.*"

And while this post-meno-mom takes the baby's crying like a trooper, Clare sees that the second-in-command, Mr. Lindy, is writing a note using the top of the birdcage as a desk. The louder the baby cries, the faster he writes, while his pigeons pace their cage, giving rapid jerks of their heads. Then he puts the pen down, stoops, and lifts a bird out of the cage. He carries it to the back door, fiddling with the bird's leg and attaching the note. Then he opens the door. Lets the bird go. Turns and skips down the hall, waving his arms wide for his child. Clare gratefully gives up the twisting baby. Lindy holds his child in an antiquated Doc Spock style and then starts shuffling his feet. Clare doesn't recognize the old man's steps. Free-form soft shoe? The child quiets. Then Lindy begins singing, "Crazy feet . . . Daddy's got Fred's crazy feet . . ."

Clare has no idea who Fred is, but I know Lindy means a dancer named Fred Astaire. As Lindy does *crazy feet,* the ceiling is creaking above their heads, as if the second-floor dwarf were standing up there swaying in time to Lindy's shuffle. Then the old man says, "All over now." And gives the quiet child back to Clare and leaves down the hall.

Clare bites her lips and starts to pinch the baby again. Suddenly piano music is banging out back, and before Clare knows what she's doing, she shifts the weight on the baby's bottom and jumps down the step into the living room. The nanny begins swaying side to side, dancing the baby.

Then she immediately stops. *What's going on, you little sack of rot? You are making me act crazy.*

And the baby smiles. Gets a glint of something. Then it happens. Clare, who by both training and inclination (not to mention pharmaceutical reinforcement) has never been moved by a baby, finds herself captured by Soda's gaze.

And the nanny suddenly loves this craphole-in-diapers. Clare's heart expands with inspired love. If she were a Persian poet she'd begin writing verse about *the companion.*

Not that Clare is feeling the corny Gerber love that unarmed amateurs engage in. No. And this isn't some captivated-by-the-dilated-pupil biological response hot-wired into our brains (nature had to prevent those Phoenicians from sacrificing infants to Baal somehow).

The love Clare feels is not even a bad case of nanny burnout.

Instead, imagine that something like a funnel has been plugged into Clare's heart, allowing a state of adoration to fill up inside her. The baby pours in grace.

Oh God, the images she is seeing!

I feel ecstatic watching Clare's face. My feelings toward her are as strong as hers toward that baby. The only difference is psychedelic: Clare is an anti-image in my skull — a vapor that keeps the rider-with-the-sickle at bay, i.e., I won't die as long as I'm near her. But to Clare, her feelings toward the baby are as solid as sculpture. It's a metal funnel that's plugged into her heart. It is Clare's fancy that it's slim like an old-fashioned ear trumpet. An elongated cone. Yes. A cone is leading out of her heart. And this baby is pouring unadulterated empathy up to the brim. Clare can think of only one name for this experience: *Cone Heart.*

Then: *Oh shit, a nanny could get arrested for this!* She whips her head up to Mrs. Lindy — but the old lady looks unconcerned.

"I'll take Soda now," the mother says calmly.

Clare actually pulls the child away. "Oh, I'll put the baby in the crib for you, Mrs. Lindy."

"No. I'll take Soda with me." The woman grabs the child. "Baby likes hearing Mommy sing."

Sing? What a couple — the singing and dancing Lindys. Then Clare hears Mr. Lindy in the garage, yelling over the piano and clapping, "One, two, three. One, two, three." Clapping? Who is playing the piano? Then Mrs. Lindy is talking. "I'm always so amazed when I see Soda's eyes closed. Little Soda was born with open eyes." She pauses, then whispers, "Just like the Buddha or a saint."

Clare has nothing to say to that.

Mrs. Lindy now peers at the nanny with a regal stance. It

occurs to Clare that in some alternate universe, Helen of Troy, Cleopatra, and Marie Antoinette have all lived to be as old as this woman, their severe beauty transformed into the same aged, iconic grace. Madame Lindy now looks away and carries her saintly Baby Buddha through the living room, down the back hall. Opens a door. Shuts it.

Clare stands there looking at the knob. *Wait a minute. What just happened?* She whips out her stash and quickly inhales an extra pinch of Vengeance. *My God. I actually bonded with that child!* If she didn't need Vengeance so bad, she'd run into the bathroom and throw up. Instead, she stands cross-armed by the closed door, shaking. At least all the Lindys appear to want her for is to guard the baby. No surprise. Geriatrics have the highest percentage of babynapping — armed nannies are necessities, not luxuries. Still, why aren't the Lindys paranoid about intruders? Visitors seem to come and go.

"Lovely Soda is in danger," she says. Then she jumps. *Lovely?* Suddenly her nanny drug hits her brain stem and she scrunches her face up, chanting, "Rug rat. Rug rat. Rug rat. Rug rat."

Breath.

"I want to kill something."

She says this and is startled by her voice. As if answering her, the old woman begins singing from inside the room. Or something akin to singing. God, Mrs. Lindy has a painful voice . . . where's the Novocain! Clare can't make out the alleged tune, but it seems familiar somehow. What language is she singing in? Not English. Or Japanese. Clare lives on the Lower East Side, and this is no Latin tongue. The nanny shakes her head, then whips the Glock from her holster. Puts it back. Whips it out again. She knows there's nothing around to shoot, but her trigger finger has started tingling. It's actually gotten physically hotter than the rest of her hand. She begins practicing her draw — Glock in, Glock out.

Glock, what a dumb name — sorry, Gaston: You were a hell of a gunsmith, but consider the chunkiness of your name versus your gun's sleek shape. I suppose this lexical conflict gives the heater a charm. It's like saying the word *Buddha* — what a chunky name for such a beneficent deity (born with open eyes no less!). Finally if any of you Ishmaels are firearm fanatics, you'll be interested to learn that Clare packs a Model 30, considered the Hope diamond of Glocks. When nannies get together and compare their firearms, Clare likes to purr, "See this delicious milled slot on the barrel and slide? Almost no muzzle jump."

And now here's Clare *doin' the Glock* — practicing her draw. Listening to the piano stopping and starting from the dance studio. Now there's Mr. Lindy doing the ivory and clapping and counting. How does he do all three at once? Suddenly, Mrs. Lindy opens the door, and Clare fakes her draw into a languid stretch.

"The milk wagon comes by at twelve," Mrs. Lindy says.

"All right," Clare says. "How is Soda?" She peers over the old woman's shoulder. Sees a simple room: a table, a music stand. The child is asleep in a large Moses cradle sitting on the floor. "Should I check and see if the baby needs changing?"

"Soda is fine. Let me get you some money and an umbrella." Clare glances out the window. "It's not raining."

"The umbrella isn't for rain," the old woman says and hands Clare a Japanese paper parasol, the thing thickly lacquered and painted dollar green. "Noon to four are peak bird hours."

"Oh, I thought life was slower out here in Jersey," Clare says.

"No," Mrs. Lindy says. "Our sky is as busy as in that Lon Chaney movie where he plays a rabbi who raises pigeons."

"He plays a Chinaman," Clare says.

"Oh, silent movies are too modern for me," she says. "But did you know that his second wife was a failed singer?"

"Whose second wife?" Clare asks.

"Lon Chaney's."

"Failed in what way?"

"She was a washed-up singer who hit the bottle. The gin bottle. Then went into a theater where a Chaney flicker was playing and drank a bottle of mercury to kill herself."

Clare gives Mrs. Lindy a long *Are you cuckoo?* look and almost says, "Is that what happened to your voice — you pulled a Mrs. Chaney?" But then the nanny decides to stay clammed. She hesitates at the door. How can Jersey be as bad as Midtown? Clare leaves the house.

Oh ornithology!

The nanny is forced to hurry under the trees, opening her umbrella just as dense streams of neo-pigeons begin crisscrossing the sky. These Jersey heavens seem as dense as the ones above Fifth Avenue and Forty-seventh. Even if you've never been to New York, you've surely gazed up at some metro sky and seen it opaque with neo-pigeons. Postmodern carrier pigeons. Did you know that real carrier pigeons became extinct right after World War I? It was only ten years ago they were genetically resurrected by Sharper Image. Think of all those messages now being borne by bird today — winging uptown, downtown, over to the tenderloin, across the causeway. All that text above our streets!

Clare follows Mrs. Lindy's verbal directions and ends up at the Reagan Monument. I've heard of the Mon, as it's called, but this is the first time I've actually sheldraked it. The Mon is hyped as the metro region's supreme fertility hoop — the stone bench that rings the base of the obelisk seems more crowded than any of the fertility hoops in Central Park. Dozens of girls are huddling there in their ponchos, sliding their bare feet on the lawn. I've heard that out in California, men are the ones who do the sitting, but women sit here in the East — supposedly the magnetic field between the marble hoop and the dirt makes a girl's eggs predatory beyond belief.

Near the base of the fertility hoop, a milk wagon stands in a puddle of melted ice, cartons covered with a plastic tarp. Don't you wonder why the Japanese insist on pulling their wagons with their foreheads? The Koreans in Manhattan must have taught them.

Clare pays for a bottle of moo.

Ten minutes later, the nanny returns swinging a milk bottle. She sees the front curtains at Big Pink move. Although Clare has never officially sheldraked, she now gets a Kathleen Keegan vibe.

What's the Irish Boss doing here?

The front door opens and an older woman walks out. Clare goes, *Yup. It's Kathleen Keegan.* President of the Nanny Broker Company. I myself do a few *Holy cows!* because I know this woman — although I have not seen her in thirty years. We had encounters when I was a boy — I'll tell you about them later. Now, my thinking follows Clare's: *What's Keegan here for?* The woman is dressed in a dark blue coat. Simple cut, not Lit Wear. Keegan is around Mrs. Lindy's age, but has a softer, less brittle charm. Keegan's gray Louise Brooks bangs are smooth, the skin along her mouth even smoother.

Clare hardens her face, wonders if Cone Heart shows.

Keegan helps Clare hoist in her bumbershoot. "Cancer-and-Christ, I hate birdshit umbrellas," she swears.

Clare gives a slight smile at this medical blasphemy. Keegan was raised a Christian Scientist, the pagan island of Ireland spawning a substantial population of Mary Baker Eddy followers.

On the Lindy porch, Keegan says, "I couldn't brief you yesterday, Clare, because a den of babynappers was discovered holing up in the Flatiron Building and I had to make sure my girls drilled every last one."

Clare hugs her milk bottle and wonders why Keegan would have to hold a briefing about anything. Does Keegan know about Cone Heart? Is this what the boss lady needs to warn her about? It comes to Clare that the Nanny Broker Company was where Mr. Lindy sent the bird this morning — although only the Devil and Kathleen Keegan could have raced their carriages through the Lincoln Tunnel so quickly!

"I came out here to make sure things go smoothly," Keegan continues. "I know Mrs. Lindy can be difficult. She has the tendency to be . . ."

Clare finishes the sentence. "Aristocratic?"

Keegan shakes her head. "No, birdbrained."

"Let me toot up before I go inside," Clare says, slipping out her tin of Vengeance. Keegan looks away as the younger nanny sniffs a hit. Clare wipes her nose and stashes the box. In her rookie days, she'd always offer the first hit of Vengeance to her boss. A respect thing. But Keegan always declined. Clare was dejected, thinking it had something to do with the unworthiness of a novice nanny. Then an experienced girl told her, "Boss is clean."

Guns are another story. In fact, the boss adores firearms. Here on the front porch of the Lindys, Keegan slips out a shiny Colt

Diamond. "Sweet savior," she coos to Clare. "Have you ever seen anything sweeter?"

"It's more petite than a Python," Clare says. She opens her gun hand. "May I?"

"Be my guest," Keegan says, a slight lilt to her voice. "Now there is a grip that was meant to fit a maiden's hand." Keegan raises her palm. "Or a nanny's."

The gun feels serious to Clare, but she still prefers her Glock. "Thank you," she says with a slight quiver in her voice.

"Thank the gun, not me," Keegan says.

Clare looks embarrassed, tries to hand the gun back. Keegan doesn't reach. Instead she says, "When I was a little girl back in Ireland, we had an old hound. Mother hated the beast, and when he got too old, she handed my father his gun case and just said, 'Finally.'" Keegan now reaches out for her Diamondback. "Father walked the dog out back by the turf huts. I waited for the shot, but it didn't come." She pauses, looking down at her gun. "At the end of the day, Father returned with the animal, saying, 'I just couldn't do it.'" Keegan now looks painfully nostalgic. "My father was deaf, you know, so he said it, 'Ah jez kud'n do't.' I held out my hand and took the gun. Father wasn't sure what I wanted it for. I led the dog out to the field. The gun was a Colt much like this. My mother later told me that the moment she heard the shot my father jumped." Keegan looks into Clare's eyes. "If you remember, my father was deaf. . . ."

"The angels singing will sound like gunfire," Clare says. *God, where did that come from? I sound like some frontier Mormon.*

"Next time we're at the office, I'll show you Father's gun," Keegan says, pocketing the Diamondback. "Now, let's go inside and placate that Lindy bitch."

. . .

The bitch in question is waiting in the front hall.

"Clare is a top-dog nanny," Keegan announces to Mrs. Lindy. "You should have seen her on last month's job — there she was, giving the baby its bottle, when this pair of babynappers broke through the door. But Clare switched the milk for her Glock and brought both 'nappers down. Not to bore you with wound ballistics, but all of my girls have a penetration range of at least twelve inches of soft tissue, so rest assured those dogs went down dead. And the shooting done, Clare finished giving the baby its bottle."

Mrs. Lindy seems impressed with this story. Clare stands trying to look pleasant, but God how she hates the telling — she's a markswoman, not a trigger-happy child-care junkie.

"I'll put the milk away and check the baby," she says and heads to the nursery first. The crib is empty. She turns, but there's Keegan behind her.

"Where's the little shit?" Clare asks, the S-word just coming out, making Clare smile. *Baby blaspheming, what a relief!*

"Sweetie has Soda," Kathleen Keegan says.

"Who?" Clare asks.

"Mr. Lindy," Keegan says.

Sweetie? What's going on here?

"I think this situation is going to work out, but . . . ," the woman says, moving close — nothing pleasant about the tone of her voice now. "You'll think this is out of line considering your skills, but I want you to be careful about bonding with Soda."

Clare imagines that her jaw has just fallen off her head.

Keegan's own jaw stays steady. "You already did, didn't you?"

Clare starts sweating again. "No, no. Of course not."

How can I explain Cone Heart?

Keegan frowns, then laughs. "Look, be careful with this little snake." She starts fishing in her purse. "Sniff an extra pinch of Vengeance, then just remember to automatically lizard-shift your eyes whenever you're with the baby." She takes out an eyescope. "Let's check your sight lines."

Clare almost snorts, but stops. "Honestly, Ms. Keegan. I don't think this is necessary. You want to check my Glock as well?"

Keegan shakes the eyescope. "Damn! The batteries are dead." She looks at Clare exasperated. "Those thieving bootleggers! Do you know how much I pay for batteries?"

Clare gives her boss a sympathetic smile. "It's okay. Just watch." She shifts her eyes lizard style, back and forth, back and forth. Remember your caretaker doing that, Ishmaels? She may not have carried a gun, but she never looked you straight in the eye. I bet you sneaked a peek or two through a child-care textbook — saw all those pages of iguanas and geckos blankly staring with beady eyes. Jesus! What a trip! Zoology 101. Can you believe today's nannies are actually tested on how fast they can dart their eyes away from a baby's? God forbid anyone should be enraptured by those dilated pupils.

But maybe we're all just prisoners of science these days: You. Me. And Clare. We're all told that current electricity is life's only supreme mystery, while God, Love, and Beauty can be explained by science. The father of Allissa, my third wife, once told me that the universal principles of feminine beauty were hardwired into men's brains. He and I would share a bottle and ponder his daughter's swan throat. Her narrow jaw. High cheekbones. All more important than her coffee-cup eyes. Even that old haute couture genius Charles Darwin claimed that nature favored beauty. But how does all this explain a woman who is unconventionally beautiful?

How does it explain Clare?

What neuron in a man's brainpan allows him to appreciate this gun-toting kitten when she gives her curious Cheshire Cat grin below her deliciously troubled eyes? Shouldn't Clare unleash evolutionary chaos?

Apparently not. And her boss finds her eyes scientifically sound as well — "Okay. You're fine, Clare."

The girl drops her shoulders.

"I would have popped you if you weren't," Keegan says.

Clare shoots her a glance — that trigger-happy old woman may or may not have been joking. As Keegan puts the useless eye-scope back in her bag, Clare notices her boss is also carrying a Ziploc filled with pink sugar cubes. Narcotics? What a surprise! So much for the boss always being clean. But what's Keegan's dope? Vengeance is never pink. No one does LSD anymore, and if they did, they'd slip blotter acid under their tongues. What is this stuff? (Note, Ishmaels, that I can't tell either — it's hell sheldraking altered states.)

The old woman looks up, gives Clare a cold smile. "Remember, Soda is a toxic baby — psychic cyanide."

Clare flicks open her compact. "All babies are poison," she mutters, before sniffing her twelfth pinch of Vengeance.

Clare spends the rest of the day with the baby — "Sweetie's child." But Soda has no influence. Of course, Clare has to slip into the bathroom more often than usual to cut a few lines. Her face is beet red near the end of her shift, and she's sweating. At five, she is about to change the baby when the child begins pawing the air and wiggling. She leans her head down and whispers, "Stop it, shit bird."

Then Clare becomes aware that her nose is changing: The baby swats it and the nanny has a beak. Like a finch. Then she has a snout — first a dog's, now a horse's. This is going on inside Clare's head, mind you. And when the nanny realizes she is twitching her nose like some cottontail bunny, she throws the baby into the crib. Then she runs to the bathroom and splashes cold water on her face.

OD'ing and hallucinating on Vengeance is one thing, but in the middle of the night back on the New York side, Clare actually dreams about the baby.

Oh, I know you're thinking, Back up, Dylan. Am I trying to slip a dream sequence by you? Yes! Clare dreamed. Do you? Ha! Sheldraking is one thing, but most of you don't even believe dreams exist — to hell with any aboriginal dreamtime. I know an Ishmael who claims that dreaming was the real Morphic/Quantitative Aberration that made electricity vanish. Not dreaming per se, but Sigmund Freud sitting down and writing *The Interpretation of Dreams* was such an affront against the sacrosanctity of humanity's mass unconscious that the electrons in AC/DC began running faster than light. At first, only criminal electrons did the speeding. Electricity appeared to work fine, it taking decades for the damage to begin. Twenty-five years after Freud, Bob Dylan could still write about having 115 dreams per night. While a Dylan born today only has four or five dreams during a lifetime.

Clare herself has dreamed twice before. Those nocturnal hallucinations occurred when she was a child. Her dream couplet lacked imagery and narration. All she remembers is that she had performed some repetitive action — like folding something over and over again.

"Mom's costumes," Clare guessed at the time, referring to the simple costumes her mother wore to do performance pieces in SoHo art galleries.

And tonight's baby dream is similar in its repetitiveness. Clare is disgusted. Dreaming of baby is the most shameful thing she has ever done. She'll never tell anyone. (I only know about it because I'm still sheldraking Clare like crazy. I'm afraid to let her out of my mind. I don't want to see the Black Rider again.) Out of respect to Clare, I won't report the dream to you except to say it involved nothing more complicated than rocking a cradle.

Nevertheless, Clare is freaked. Burned. "I dreamed about a baby," she repeats over and over, hugging her stomach. It hurts.

As for me — I mainline Clare all night. The Black Rider aside, it's kinda fun keeping Clare on my mind. It's like I'm some sort of goofy teenager again. I told you that I have business with the Lindy guy, but I'll brood about him later. All I care about is Clare. At sunrise, I sheldrake the nanny is wearing a subdued Lewis Carroll / White Rabbit number. Aren't babies murder on white? Yes, but that's how a nanny keeps her edge. Keegan calls white "the alert color — white like powdered Vengeance." As for alert fashion — I exalt Clare in white. White makes her face more confrontational, more out there, as they say.

A few hours later, Clare does a shaky snort of Vengeance as she walks by the Mon. She notes that there must have been some wear-white resonance vibrating through the area this morning, as most of the sitters are wearing white too. (Forget what old feminists say — red doesn't make you more fertile.) At Big Pink, Mrs. Lindy lets Clare in, and the old woman is wearing a bone-colored non-Lit skirt, her arms behind her back tying the belt. The nanny notes that the small pouch is still strung around the old woman's neck. "Good. You're prompt," Mrs. Lindy says. "I have singing class today and must practice."

"You teach singing?" Clare asks.

Mrs. Lindy puts her hand to her chest. "Me? No. I'm a student."

There's something humble about this gesture — Clare is touched. Then curious. *What's in the pouch?* I zero in on it, but I can't tell what's inside either. It's just a simple cameo kind of thing in plain white fabric.

"Do you want me to stand guard while you sing with the baby?" Clare asks.

"Oh, no. I need to sing alone this morning," Mrs. Lindy answers. "I'm going to reach some high ones and I don't want to hurt Soda."

Hurt? Mrs. Lindy sings that shrilly?

The old artist says no more. Clare wonders if the pouch is full of herbs for her voice. The mother disappears into her singing room, while Clare pauses at the door to the nursery. She takes a deep breath, then walks in. The baby sees her and begins hollering loud syllabic baby talk from the crib.

"Can it," Clare mutters, and pinches Soda's jaw. Hard. Harder. By the time the baby starts crying, Clare has left red marks. Unprofessional. Then, what's this? The child is lying below a bonding mobile, but it's an outdated one with little plastic circles. This wasn't here yesterday. Bunnies on one side. Photos of the Lindys on the other. The Lindys are roughly ten years younger in the pictures, and Clare examines them more closely. Mr. Lindy's *American Gothic* essence is a bit softened with youth, while Mrs. Lindy looks almost glamorous in her turban and jewels.

Clare doesn't get it. And neither do I. This mobile makes no sense, because obviously a baby is supposed to bond with the parents as the parents are, not as they once were. Clare shrugs and struggles with the dropside of the crib, doing the lizard with her sight line as Soda begins kicking and screaming harder.

(God, this lizarding — this constant shifting of the glance — is a killer on a girl's eyes. No wonder nannies perversely become *Un Chien Andalou* fanatics — cranking through that silent movie's razor-to-eyeball scene — it reminds them of training!)

Abruptly the baby goes quiet. Now the house seem too still and Clare reaches for her Glock. Then she hears a *fa-fa-fa* in some faraway room. She wonders if the singing is coming from upstairs or down. She goes into the hallway, cocking her head. Yup — Mrs. Lindy is singing, the door shut. Clare returns to the nursery.

And draws her artillery for real.

A man is standing over the bunny crib, staring at the bonding mobile.

He glances up. An Asian. She is surprised that she didn't immediately shoot him. Probably because he's giving off such peculiar resonance. She is sure that he's Japanese — the palest Asian she has ever seen. He is decked out in total Jap Noir. Ultra beat. She would bet that he's a hotshot burando from Fukuchiyama. Or an art student from Musabi. Could he be the pacing neighbor from upstairs? No. She would have heard him come down.

"Who are you?" she asks.

He replies in a high, almost genderless voice, "I am See-Sarr."

What kind of name is that? He looks like a Kenji or Yasujiro. He smiles and asks, "Gonna shoot me?"

She doesn't answer.

The Asian lifts a British-sized teacup to his lips — Clare sees that he's wearing black riding gloves. Gloves make her think of fingers. Fingers make her think of the piano. *Ah ha,* Clare concludes. A Japanese pianist. Lindy must clap and See-Sarr plays and the Japanese dancers dance. But she frowns: See-Sarr as a name doesn't sound right.

I'll tell you all now that his name sounds fine — it's just not a Japanese one. The problem is that Clare is thinking in Japanese. A week from now, Clare will be eating a salad and think, "Oh, my God! His name is Caesar."

The dainty china he is pinching is not full of Darjeeling, but java — Clare smells it. There's a faint steam. Idiot! He'll scald the baby! She moves right next to the man, leaning forward so he'll have to step away. But he doesn't. He just stands there, cup steaming. Their bodies are so close, her breast touches the brim of his cup. She feels the heat. She knows before she looks that there will be a stain on her White Rabbit.

Clare stiffens her back. Extends her head. You could say she's towering over this Japanese man. Then she says the single word, "Move." The Japanese pianist may have the passive interest of an animal sniffing wood, but Clare has the stance of a gunwoman herding the target to a more convenient place where she can shoot him.

And that's what she's going to do. Her gun hand starts rhythmically shaking, while she starts jerking her head in a circle.

Vengeance.

Vengeance.

The drums start beating.

She wants to shoot him. She's going to do it. Just look at the guy. Nonchalantly staring down at his coffee. His gloves. She is suddenly aware of a soft scraping sound above her head — someone is slowly dragging a heavy bag across the floor.

Clare hears a sudden high-pitched opera note — a woman's voice. Then the baby gives a brief *whah!* There's a thump above her head — running footsteps. As Caesar moves, the baby stirs. Clare holsters her gun and lifts Soda from the crib. "It's cool. Shut up. Shut up, you." Then Clare turns as the Japanese pianist slips out the door. A beat later, Mrs. Lindy sticks her head in. "I forgot to tell you that the milk wagon is early on Tuesdays."

"Okay," Clare says. She lays Soda back into the crib.

"Oh, no," the woman coos. "Mommy will take little Soda." Then she loses her breath — her expression goes gray.

"Are you okay, Mrs. Lindy?"

"Yes." The old woman laughs. Clare notices the pouch is now in Mrs. Lindy's hand — the woman herself just cooing at Soda. "Mommy just hit a high note."

Then she looks surprised. "Oh! Let me get you some money."

Mrs. Lindy places the pouch beside the bunny lamp, then fishes in the pockets of her dress. "Damn. Just a minute."

The old woman leaves the room carrying Soda. What a taunt. Clare refuses to pick the pouch up. She looks away and for the first time notices that all the bunnies in this room have Asian eyes. She turns back and reaches out to the pouch and squeezes it. It feels full of small brittle nuggets.

Clare peels open the pouch. Jesus Christ — teeth! The pouch is full of teeth. Small. Yellowed with age. A shine on them, like pieces of coral. What animal are they from? They're not sharp enough to be dog canines. Baby teeth? Shit yes! The old woman wears a pouch full of baby teeth around her neck.

Five minutes later, Clare leaves the house on a milk run. Caesar is following. Why? To watch his coffee spot dry? He's wearing a black beret. If Clare were a bird — what a target it would make.

"It looks like rain," he says in Japanese.

Clare refuses to chat about the weather. "What's with the baby teeth?" she asks. In English.

For one moment Caesar widens his eyes. "You know about the baby?"

"What baby?"

"The one born with teeth."

"What are you talking about? Babies aren't born with teeth."

Caesar peers at her. "Not always true. Napoleon was born with teeth. Jimi Hendrix too."

Clare scowls. What is he talking about?

Now he's pointing. "There's my dude."

Dude? A man sporting a shaved crown and dreadlocks is slouching near the obelisk. The jiving Japanese jaunts over to the guy — "his dude" — but they refrain from slapping high five. Instead, Caesar slips out a wallet and begins counting bills. The dude looks uncomfortable at this public show of payment. But Caesar tallies the bills at his leisure, signaling for the dude to display his wares. The other frowns, but opens a cooler packed with flashlight batteries. Kneeling, Caesar chooses a dozen — testing each one by licking the tip.

Yech! You don't lick your watts, do you? It's a myth that your tongue tastes the voltage. Back in those Eveready days, batteries were filled with copper and acid, but our black market batteries are made of fermented compost.

That's cowshit in my book.

On the walk back to Big Pink, Clare can't resist saying, "I've been gypped plenty by dead batteries, but I'll never put the things in my mouth." She unconsciously puckers her lips. "It's a dignity first, hygiene second issue."

"You suck nanny dope and I suck volts — what's the difference?" Caesar asks.

Clare frowns, then blows him a kiss. Oh! This is one of those moments that makes sheldraking so fulfilling. . . . Look at that nanny's kisser! Clare's mouth reminds me of the 1866 beauty book that inspired my father when he was designing Lit Wear, *The Lepwolf Guide to Comeliness.* In its pages young ladies were advised that they could achieve delicate "rosebud" lips by repeating words beginning with P — *peaches, prisms, papa* — over and over for an hour a day.

What crazy words did Clare chant as a girl? I go off in my own little dream space and see images of lips circling the void.

Back in New Jersey, it's started raining as the two return to the Lindy house. Clare hears the old mom suddenly do-re-mi-ing in the singing room. Then she notices Mr. Lindy out the back window. He's in the courtyard — holding Soda in one hand and an umbrella in the other, doing his albino soft shoe. Clare heads out the back door, but ends up in a storeroom full of grocery boxes, book boxes — all likely filled with dead appliances, cords carefully separated as lines in a parachute. A second door leads to the courtyard where Mr. Lindy is dancing. Soda stays perfectly quiet. The only sound is Daddy's fencing shoes squishing in the grass.

"I'll take the baby, Mr. Lindy," she calls. "Soda shouldn't be out in the wet." *We wouldn't want the little rodent to catch cold, would we?*

Mr. Lindy looks at her sideways. There's rain on the old hoofer's glasses — but strangely enough, the baby seems dry. Completely dry. Soda's eyes have shrunken pinprick pupils. Lizard pupils. Lizard baby. The Vengeance is kicking in good — this baby makes Clare fantasize about being a Roman legionnaire boogeying at a Slaughter of the Innocents party. The piano begins pounding from the dance studio. "I have to go," Mr. Lindy says, and just hands Clare the baby.

"The umbrella!" she calls.

He pauses. Is he actually considering whether to give it to her or not? Clare just grabs the thing, noticing that Soda feels heavier now, more like a baby.

Ah, would serve you right if you drowned, little turd of misery.

The nanny looks down and sees Soda give a sudden yawn — a big baby yawn conveying innocence, a yawn that gently stretches the contours of the innocent's chubby face. The yawn finished, Soda looks up at Clare with eyes that suddenly seem neither Occidental nor Asian, but eyes abruptly round like those on Japanese comic book characters. Clare extends her free hand to slap the baby and get it going, when the child gives yet another wide terrier yawn and — oh! — the baby's pupils become lovely dilated orbs. What peepers! Without warning, Clare feels the surging presence of this other life — this fellow animal — and an overwhelming sense of *I will protect you, little one. Clare will protect you.* After all, she is big and can talk, and this other is small and silent, but — oh! — this other knows the small mammal things beyond speech. This is equipoise.

It's Cone Heart.

Again.

She holds the baby closer and finds herself saying, "Little dear one. Little dear one."

Then she has an idea that is totally startling. Totally out of keeping for a nanny high on Vengeance. This baby would be worth crossing the desert for. She can imagine kneeling in the stable hay and murmuring moos to behold a baby like this, to honor Soda's state of babyness — that state all of us are in exile from. Yes. Clare could kneel in a stable for the Lindy baby. Or kneel in the rain. As Clare starts to crouch right there outside Jersey Bounce Studio, I consider her imagery.

Would I cross the desert for Clare?

Well, sure. But I can't really clothe myself in her imagery. My feelings toward Clare are not parallel to Cone Heart. Clare won't die without the baby, but I'm not sure I can say the same about me denied Clare.

And I see Clare kneeling with the baby. Then the nanny notices Mrs. Lindy in the storeroom.

Oh shit! I'm caught! She'll tell!

Clare straightens and hurries out of the rain with the baby. But apparently Soda's mother didn't notice. Mrs. Lindy is in the middle of fishing through a box, then quickly covers the lid with *Hide it! Hide it!* body language. The woman now reaches for her baby. "Mommy is going to be singing this morning. Eureka is coming. Isn't that nice?"

But Clare doesn't hand the kid over — *No. No. No. I'll not give you my baby!* Then she recovers. And carefully hands Mommy her child. The nanny strains to deaden her face. *I'm probably grinning like an idiot.*

Mrs. Lindy leaves the storeroom with Soda, while Clare

stands there in a stupor. Then she starts to shake. *I'm longing for Soda worse than Vengeance.*

Clare starts hissing curses about drug baby. China white baby. Candy baby. Baby like a bankroll.

This is crazy.

She has to get out of here. Go somewhere and tie one on. Or better yet, head to the Avenue B gun club and unload a clip. And then figure out how to get off this job.

Clare stares at Mrs. Lindy's clandestine box. She opens the cardboard container. It's full of LPs — not sturdy gramophone disks, but flimsy vinyl from the old turntable days. What's the big deal? She doesn't recognize any of the covers. There's no Dylan or anything sixties.

She then pokes through other boxes. If you've ever dated an Allied Van man, you know that movers call this stuff chowder. The Lindys have crammed much miscellany out here.

Clare is just about to stop snooping when she finds the book box. She paws through the volumes — Calvin Klein. Versace. And sure enough, there's her father's picture on a blue spine. The title — *The Ethereal Solace of the Inside Child.* A book he wrote about a decade before the electric current died. Before General Electric was court-martialed. She slides the book out and flips through it. Yup. Passages are highlighted. Clare has never actually read the volume, but like all of us, she's absorbed its contents through the culture. She knows the pages that readers usually highlight. Page 5. Six paragraphs on 35. Top of 48. Etc. Clare doesn't know what's on these particular pages because she can't read them.

Not for any psychological reasons.

Clare just can't read.

That is to say, Clare can't read English. She was never one

of those Shaker *Logos No!* kids. While Clare's mother was doing performance art in New York City, Clare was living with her father on the other side of the planet in Japan. He had enrolled his daughter in Nagasaki Elementary first grade — "You don't want to be different from the Japanese kids, do you?"

His daughter solemnly shook her head.

By the time Clare was eight, she was writing Japanese in her needlessly locked diary (her father and his new bride, Clare's stepmother, only knew French and English). By the time Clare was ten, her teachers allowed her to skip English class under the mistaken assumption the girl had mastered writing in her mother language. To this day, Clare can't read English.

The nanny turns to leave the storeroom and trips over another bonding mobile, just sitting in a pile on the floor. She lifts it up and sees the thing has green bunny icons from twenty years ago. The Lindys are young in these photos — maybe in their late forties. Clare stares at them a long while, then continues poking around the debris. She finds more bonding mobiles. Lots. She unwraps them. Each contains headshots of the Lindys. Some have additional icons attached containing writing, which she can't, of course, read. Clare uses the ages on the pictures to sort the mobiles chronologically. Witnesses Mrs. Lindy's transformation from a young severe woman to an old severe woman while Mr. Lindy stays faithful to his *American Gothic* essence. Clare ends up unwrapping two dozen mobiles — forty years' worth of bonding. Forty years' worth of babies.

Oh God, Clare is thinking. *The Lindys are in the black market baby trade!* Then she shakes her head. Baby brokers just hang bunnies above the cribs of young product, never bonding mobiles. She finds herself muttering the words *Lindy, Lindy, Lindy.* Then it hits her that the Lindy was a dance in the 1930s. The Lindy Hop, in fact. So named after "Lucky Lindy," a.k.a. Charles Lindbergh. A famous racing car driver. No. A pilot. His plane hopped the big ditch. Then he got involved with Amelia Earhart. Wait. Clare is thinking of John Gilbert and Greta Garbo. Wait. Now she has it. What happened to Charles Lindbergh is this: He lived a hundred years ago, when nannies didn't carry gats or tommy guns. And so the man's baby son was kidnapped. And never recovered. And some poor schmuck was falsely convicted of the crime. Electrocuted, in fact! Forget Sigmund Freud's *Interpretation of Dreams.* Could that have been the Morphic Aberration that started the disappearance of electricity?

Probably not.

But even if it was, what does this have to do with the Lindys of New Jersey? Nothing. Unless the name Lindy contains Morphic Resonance that's somehow affecting their baby, Soda.

The Lindys kidnap babies?

God, these thoughts terrify the nanny. *Gimmie another hit of Vengeance.*

High noon. Clare walks into the nursery and finds Soda alone lying face-up under a bonding mobile — a new one — vigorously shaking little fists at a dozen crescent widgets containing recent photos of Mr. and Mrs. Lindy — old Pop, old Mom.

The baby stops.

"This is good-bye, dumb mammal," Clare whispers.

Why did I say that? The baby ignores her and stares up at the bonding mobile. Clare jiggles the plastic photos. "Earth to Soda. Earth to Soda. I have to quit you to preserve my hard-boiled nanny status. . . ."

Soda stares upward, and the baby's lips move as if forming words. At that moment, the upstairs dwarf/child starts typing. Clare can almost believe the neighbor is taking dictation. The typing speeds up the click-tap click-tap ringing-bell carriage-slide. Can a typist hunt-and-peck deliberately loud? Clare notes that Soda glances back at her. The nanny quickly does lizard-eyes. *No more Cone Heart for me.* But the baby cones nothing — just gives an abrupt yawn and immediately falls asleep.

"How many words are you going to type per minute when you grow up, shrimp?" Clare asks the sleeping child.

From the ceiling comes click-click thump-bing! sliding-clunk. Her father told her that in the old days, typing was almost silent — you could barely hear a Macintosh. On the way to the kitchen Clare stops by the birdcage and considers pigeons typing with their beaks. Click click click. Hunt 'n' peck.

In the kitchen it hits her: — *I can't quit today. I'll look like a flake if I just show up at the Nanny Broker Company.* Then, a new idea: *Send a message to Keegan by bird.*

"Do it," he says.

Who?

She spins. Caesar. He reaches and rummages in a tin box beside the birdcage, retrieving pen and pad.

"Not to worry," he tells her. He says this in Japanese. No smile. "Every nanny contemplates quitting by now." He says this in English. Then smiles.

Every nanny? Clare thinks. *What, the Lindys burn through a nanny a week?* And how did he know she couldn't read or write English? Clare doesn't believe in Rupert Sheldrake. Maybe ESP is a sushi thing. The nanny tells him in Japanese: "I have to get Soda . . . " and walks away. Then changes her mind. She turns and says softly, "Okay. Begin. Memo to Kathleen Keegan."

"Speak English, please."

"Your handwriting better be neat," Clare threatens. He gives a patient smile and nods. "*Dear Ms. Keegan,*" she continues. "*I feel the chemistry between me and the Lindys is not good for the baby* — no wait! Put *not suitable for the Lindys' baby.*" Clare pauses until he finishes, then dictates, "*I am requesting a substitute assignment. I've said nothing to Mr. or Mrs. Lindy about my desire.*"

Caesar stops. "Your desire?"

"Yes. My desire," she says, frowning. "*In closing, I think it would be best for all if this request* — no, wait! — *if my request for a change originated from you.*" She recites the closing, then takes a deep breath, sighs.

Clare agrees that it's a pain in the ass not being able to write in English, but her illiteracy suited her father. He cringed that his only daughter might someday read the words he wrote: *Your children will deny your Inside Child, so envision that they're really a little brother or sister. Realize your children are competition for Mom's love. Your job as a parent is to figure out what this "Mom" represents to you.*

How could he ever look his daughter in the eye if she knew he wrote this? (It never dawned on the man that his daughter paged through the Japanese translation of his book in the stalls near her pachinko parlor of choice.)

Caesar attaches the note to a bird. Clare follows him to the back door. She should be feeling hopeful about getting off this job, but something is bothering her. She sees Caesar fussing with the bird's leg.

"Watch it," the nanny scolds. "You'll damage the fowl."

"Not to worry," Caesar says, opening the door to the courtyard. He takes a step and suddenly flings the pigeon into the air. The bird's wings crackle for a moment, then it takes off.

Clare isn't thinking at all. No. She is just running back through the house, out the front door. Pumping her arms and legs, navigating on automatic pilot.

Her bird is flying above the front lawn. Her bird looks like a typographical character in Japanese. The bird is *Twachi* — the sign of longing. Without a moment's hesitation, Clare whips out her Glock and races after the pigeon, her gun arm raised.

"I can't go cold turkey. I can't go cold turkey," she chants. She realizes she means Cone Heart. She can't go cold turkey on Cone Heart.

The nanny shoots the bird out of the sky. In an explosion of blood and feathers, Clare imagines the pigeon is now spelling the word MOTHERFUCKER.

She knows how to read that American word.

When Clare returned to the States, she picked up enough English to get by. She can now read the words *name,* EXIT, *Diet Coke.* She recognizes *Bank* and *USA.* She has studied money to familiarize herself with numbers. She recognizes oft-repeated graffiti. She's always known how to read *shit, fuck, asshole.* She knows how to read *Jesus.*

Caesar says nothing about her assassination of the bird. Too bad if that fowl was his favorite. Clare sleepwalks through the rest of her shift, until the day is finally over, and she sails home to Manhattan at sunset. The nanny vows that going cold turkey off Cone Heart will be no big deal.

As for me, I worry. Although I don't specifically feel Cone Heart for Clare, what if we're linked through that phenomenon itself? If Clare removes herself from the baby, will I in turn be jettisoned from Clare? Will that Black Rider start his ride? I'll die.

I sheldrake Clare turning from the river, realizing that the deck is full of babies, but no nannies. Just mothers — *amateurs!* — with dozens of babies. Some in strollers. Some in buggies. A few slung in papoose contraptions peering over moms' shoulders. They are all staring at a solitary woman in a black leather jacket who stands on the bridge smoking furiously — hand to mouth, then suck and puff, hand to mouth again . . . Clare looks back at the babies. Double-checks to make sure none of her peers are aboard. Then does something completely unprofessional: Clare walks beside the smoker and finds herself giving each baby a wide, heartfelt smile. *I'll control Cone Heart like I control Vengeance. I'll take both on my own terms.* She beams her new state of calmness to them all. Her mind telegraphs assurances that someday they too will grow up and wear fine White Rabbits. . . .

Each and every baby takes in Clare's smile. And against all odds of pediatric physics, it happens: Each one gives a choke and begins crying. Hear that simultaneous lament! That immediate *whah!* We all know the Wailing Wall — here is the Wailing Boat, each sailor-baby directing its specific contribution to Clare, who is startled by the din, but also annoyed. Any professional could translate this crying. None of these *whahs* are about fear. Or pain. Or even discomfort. This is selfish crying from selfish babies, each one wailing a sturdy give-me-attention *whah*.

The smoking woman reacts to this noise like a signal. She

flings her butt and abruptly runs toward the other side of the boat.

The Smoker.

Clare should have radared this woman's intentions — but the nanny let herself get distracted by the din of the babies. She watches the running Smoker dip her shoulders and sweep up a doughy toddler midwail from a mother's arms, then continue dashing across the deck. Clare slips out her Glock. The drums start up, *Vengeance, Vengeance.* The nanny holds a calm draw, observing that the snatched kid is older than Soda — this toddler's eyes now wide in surprise as the Smoker wedges the baby under her left arm and holds her right arm out Ronald Reagan/ *Where iz the rest of me?* style in her race to the rail.

Clare is in predator-toying-with-mouse mode — where is the Smoker going to run to on a boat?

Big mistake. In one full motion the Smoker flings the child off the deck.

Everyone is frozen on deck — baby overboard!

Then Clare is running as the baby falls in slow motion — you Ishmaels can imagine doing downers and then cranking a silent movie frame-by-frame, watching Mary Pickford, say, crossing the Hudson — the blonde in pigtails and furry winter coat leaping the ice floes so slowly that her leap becomes an extension of your gesturing elbow.

This child moves that slowly, a slow glide above Pickford's same river. This baby is no longer crying. This baby is just assimilating its momentum. Then registering shock as it does a deadweight drop into the Hudson.

Clare has just watched a kidnapper pitch a baby away like sea trash. The nanny reaches the railing, then — ah ha! — she sees the small rowboat bobbing below the ferry. A skinny woman — nose-pegged, tattooed — balances in the center of that boat. Baby pirates? Now the baby is in that woman's arms.

And Clare carefully aims her semiautomatic. Waits for the woman to lower the child about six inches . . .

But the Smoker grabs Clare — the woman's black cowhide sleeve stiff. Creaking.

"Look out! She has a gun!" someone is screaming. Clare yells over her shoulder, "I'm a nanny, you dimwit!" and wedges her body into the Smoker's groin, smelling the woman's Pall Mall airs. Looking above the woman's leather shoulder, Clare sees the baby lying at the bow of the boat — the other woman sitting about two feet aft, frantically rowing toward Manhattan. But there's a swirl at the stern, some strange wake from a clanging buoy — the little rowboat goes nowhere. The baby starts crying again, a plaintive, seasick call that even an amateur could translate: "Mother! Oh, Mother!" Clare hears a woman answer, a soprano shrieking, "Oh my — Dylan! My Dylan!"

Ah ha. One of my clan. . . . Well, perhaps the baby pirates will give this child a new name. A preferred name. Maybe make him a little Nate.

A woman runs to the railing, surrounded by a Greek chorus of additional matriarchs. This particular Dylan's mom wears a long camel coat, the fabric bristled like fur. More Mary Pickford style than Lit Wear. The mother struggles clumsily over the railing and flops into the Hudson.

Bad move. Bad coat.

Clare and the Smoker lean further over the rail, watching the woman — impossibly weighted down by her coat — thrash in the wake, dog-paddling toward her Dylan. The kidnapper quickly stands and balances in the rowboat, gripping an oar. She almost loses her balance, but then begins swatting at the struggling woman. The first stroke misses — just splashes. The second strikes the mother's head.

Clare swings her body completely into the Smoker's, using the momentum to lean them both so far over the railing it defies physics why they don't do a dunk themselves. Instead, their bodies hug belly-to-belly — Clare's arm extending above the Smoker's head, the crook of Clare's arm pressed against the Smoker's ear.

God, Clare's body looks elegant and long stretched that way . . .

The nanny herself feels the hard nugget of the kidnapper's fertility earring. To the Smoker, it will feel as if she hears Clare's gun through the ceramic ball of that very earring. In reality, the Smoker is hearing the semiautomatic through the bones of Clare's arm — the nanny shooting the rowboat babynapper, her hand exaggerating the recoil.

Clare is surprised at how enraged she feels. So she shoots the babynapper again.

Number Two.

Then the nanny pushes back from the Smoker and jams the gun into that woman's leather jacket.

"Heather!" the Smoker is crying, waving her arms at the water. "Heather!" The Smoker's face is etched with disbelief and pain. She turns her head to Clare's, crying, "We were together before the electricity went." Then she tries scrambling over the rail.

Clare wants to say, "So what?" Instead, she puts her gun on safety and clubs the Smoker with the butt, conscious that the other mothers have crowded around them. She looks back at the river. Heather is floating on her back in the drink — arms angel-spread toward heaven. The mother is now aboard the rowboat, kneeling above her Dylan, her coat bloated and dripping water.

Mother as wet sheepdog.

It takes fifteen minutes, but a plastic ladder is lowered to Dog Mom and her babe while Clare keeps the mother-mob from lynching the Smoker. "Stand back," Clare yells. "She's mine."

The nanny's face is red. The drums recede. Suddenly the Vengeance doesn't feel right. Clare holsters her Glock and shoves the Smoker into the mothers, yelling, "Have fun, girls."

When the ferry finally docks, the nanny hurries off the boat, past the confused cops stomping up the gangplank holding their clubs and cans of riot foam. Clare heads down Fourteenth Street, but stops and grips a gaslight and starts weeping — half out of rage, the rest from confusion. *I can't believe I actually smiled at a boatload of babies!*

3 radio city overdose

AS CLARE flails away at Cone Heart, I try going cold turkey myself. Off Clare. Nix on sheldraking. I don't even muse about Clare using conventional thinking, let alone brood about her. I just go to a Times Square crank joint and watch ole Miss Egypt Death herself, Theda Bara — the original Madonna before Madonna was Madonna. Theda is a little too plump for my tastes, but I spin the crank and smile at her vamping. Then suddenly Clare appears in the viewfinder.

Wait. I'm hallucinating this. I don't have involuntary sheldrakes. And even if I did, I've never sheldraked through an external apparatus before. But I'm clearly seeing Clare in this nickelodeon. She looks too wired to sleep, so she hunts up a Kiwi tin and patiently removes the laces from both of Paramour #3's wingtips. Takes a piece of muslin — to me this woman is as lovely as some Renaissance painting of *Veronica and Her Cloth* — and smears the black wax across the left shoe's throat, its instep. A chunk of wax slips out of the tin. Close-up as it plops on her knee. Slides down her calf. I yearn to pinch that black clump with my finger and smear thick hieroglyphs up her thigh.

Long shot: the nanny abruptly rubs her eyes — so much lizarding-the-baby today. Now she has black tattoo streaks on her face. Clare stands and goes to her treadmill to try to pace up some personal volts under the troubled painted gaze of Mr. and Mrs. Gothic. Their eyes inspire the nanny to slip on a cucumber eye mask to cool her own peepers.

"Time for a little bump and grind," she says after five minutes of pacing.

Well, my interest is up, so to speak. I should tell you that I know why stripping is an occasional desire with Clare. When she was ten, her stepmother read the girl the profile of Clare's mother that had just appeared in *People* magazine. Evidently other SoHo art-mob strippers, or *ecdysiasts,* stripped while wearing monster masks or slabs of bacon, to attack the patriarchy. But ever since the Reagan-era Clare's mother had stayed true to minimalist-ritual truths by stripping as blankly as possible out of nondescript gray garments — the Performing Garage audience never remembering her skirts and blouses once they were dropped. The *People* article unfavorably contrasted Clare's mother to famous strippers such as Chesty Morgan and Watermelon Rose. Clare herself knew nothing about traditional striptease, but ever since she was five the idea of a woman doing a shimmy in a G-string seemed "Neat!"

"Grow up, Clare!" her mother scolded. "I've told you a thousand times that Roland Barthes says a G-string just turns a woman into a mineral."

Huh? The child didn't care. G-string bump and grind seemed fun, not ironic and postmodern. Clare was still thinking that at ten years old. She thinks that way now, standing before her mirror, rotating her hips, swiveling the hem of her I Could Not Stop for

Death slip. Clare has never actually heard striptease music, but she imagines it sounds like "Rainy Day Woman #12 & 35" played by John Philip Sousa. She starts humming a tune.

I shake my head. Yes! I hear her singing.

Her song sounds like "The Stars and Stripes Forever." And she suddenly flings off her eye mask.

Ah, the nanny's temples and superciliary arch aren't so swollen now. Her wise-sad eyes look up from her almost too-tiny head. I watch this woman and imagine Clare as Lon Chaney's lovely kid sister, radiant and spooky.

She gets off the treadmill, puts her arms behind her, and begins beating a rhythm on her rump through her slip. Suddenly a small black halo of five pointed stars circles her head. Are they real or a special effect in the movie? I stop the crank. Everything freezes. I now notice that Clare is wearing a pair of wingtips — when did she put them on? Even without laces, they look tight and dig into her ankles — #3 must have been a small man. To do him honor, she begins pacing on tiptoe in a tense orbit — in this vision I'm having, Clare is moving on her own — I'm not turning the crank on the viewbox. Clare is circling the table, the chair, the divan, back to the table . . .

As Clare walks, the stars get bigger and bigger around her head. Big enough that I see they aren't stars. No. They're those Muybridge images of the Black Rider. What's the Reaper doing galloping around her lovely brow?

Clare abruptly sits down at a table, drops her head in her hands. "Shit," she mutters. Then the nanny jumps up and pats the top of the icebox for her tin of Vengeance. I notice a dozen empty tins on the floor. Clare must have really been strung out about smiling at the babies — she came home and mainlined all her Vengeance. The nanny now finds the last tin. Then mutters,

"Shit," as she runs her little finger around the edges of the empty tin. Sucks the finger.

"I have to score," she sighs. "I have to score."

I realize what the horses mean. They don't really exist in any conventional way, of course. I mean Clare can never see them. And none of you Ishmaels will ever see them. But I see them. I saw them by sheldraking. And they circle Clare's head. What this means is: The nanny will die if she doesn't get more Vengeance.

I watch her throw on a ratty old cotton Far from the Madding Crowd and head out the door.

A junkie's hurry. She's even left her Glock. . . .

In the nickelodeon, I'm spinning my arm so fast that the other customers have backed away from my crank box. I see Clare on her street. I see her flag down an uptown Dead of Night trolley on Avenue A. I know Washington Square Park shuts down at midnight, so I bet she'll head up to Radio City to connect with a dealer.

She's riding knee-to-knee with lantern-light workers and a motley crew of Tattoo Boys all strapped in The Horror, the Horror Conrads. She tries chatting them up, hoping no one will notice she has the heebee-jeebies. She thinks that she's been chattering away for the last four blocks, but everyone is ignoring her. Then the nanny realizes her utterances have occurred only in her head.

It's suddenly pitch-black outside. She presses her face to the window and sees the carriage is now north of the Con Ed Building, where there are no gaslights. No lanterns shine. The horses do a spooked trot and the passengers go quiet. "I hear that this lack of light above Fourteenth Street is a form of public support for Con Ed," Clare says to the Mott boy across the aisle. "Residents voluntarily leave the boulevard dark to exhibit their faith that Con Ed will someday bring the current back."

The young hood yawns and scratches the crotch of his Conrads, laughing. "Mistah Kurtz, he dead."

My poor junkie, Clare! If I were a rider I could inform the nanny that her speech was a nice conceit but untrue. I know this because my fourth wife worked for the city and told me those blackened blocks are just a result of municipal shortcomings.

Ah. Park Avenue South has plenty of light. Clare's trolley trots west to Fifth, the avenue lined with hieroglyph lights — white-green kerosene glare shining through glass layered with graffiti. They trot uptown through a glowing corridor. Clare rings the bell fifty blocks later at Saks. Steps off. Everyone figures she's going to one of those all-night appliance stores where the faithful kneel in front of the big stuff like refrigerators and pray, but she walks through a promenade over to Radio City.

Good. Her dealer hangs out there. She'll live through this night.

Ishmaels, if you've never been to New York, know that Radio City is a three-block complex of skyscrapers surrounding a central plaza — that space watched over by a giant naked man, an Art Deco Prometheus covered in gold leaf. My father told me the god was originally modeled after a Caucasian politician named Nelson Rockefeller. In the days of wires and sockets, this Nelson gazed down upon an ice-skating rink. My father used to skate here. I can close my eyes and still see Dad doing lazy circles as he brooded about Lit Wear pleats and buttonholes. He brought me with him to run wild through the General Electric Building. Yes — General Electric! There was so much free-flowing current at Radio City that my father even skated here at night. Now the skyscrapers are strictly Frankenstein's castle. Without electricity and an ice rink, this plaza is useless. They burn raw cedar pikes from dusk to dawn to keep wild animals away. Clare walks under these glorified tiki lights searching for a dealer. The horses circling her head are starting to blur in a continuous motion. A black halo of trotting Reaper. This woman needs Vengeance bad. But the street is empty. No dealers. She circles the block. Not even pedestrians. *There's never a dealer around when you need him. . . .*

There's only one thing to do. Clare figures she'll slip up to the Nanny Broker office and jimmy the storage cabinet. Pilfer some Vengeance. She walks to the GE Building's service entrance on Forty-ninth Street. Music thuds inside, but she sees the guard is gone — just a lantern and gramophone on an empty desk, music hiked up loud, the spinning platter playing some old-time misogynist rap: *Beat your woman till she sneezes / Beat your woman till she sneezes.* As the music plays, I see the horses get bigger. Their hoofbeats become the funk beat on the platter. Their flanks obscure Clare's head as she hurries in and heads through the old elevator lobby, fishing through her purse for her keys. At the other end of the hall, we hear a man yelling, "Hey! Hey you! What you want?" Clare ignores him — she can't leave a record of her dead-of-night visit: nannies have nothing but contempt for colleagues who wig out in public, desperate for a fix. Clare unlocks a stainless-steel door leading to a stairwell. Shuts the door. Dark — total noir! Where are the horses now? If light can be sucked into darkness by gravity, Clare is now in the belly of a collapsed star. But smears of orange mark her vision. These marks are real — but not photons of light. They're latent lantern glare impressed on her retinas.

The woman reaches for her shoes.

"Jesus," she mutters, feeling Paramour #3's wingtips. *I forgot I had these on.* She now is running silently up the stairs barefoot, holding the shoes in one hand, feeling her way along the railing with the other. She's been here before. The stairway goes thirteen steps up — then turns right and up another thirteen, then a door and another set of steps. These stairs lead all the way to the seventieth floor — 1,820 steps. When Clare reaches a landing, she counts off: "First floor . . . second floor . . . third floor. . . ." The nanny is heading for the seventh. As she climbs she realizes how wet with sweat her I Could Not Stop for Death blouse has become. How shaky her hands are. *If I don't get some Vengeance I die,* she says to herself. And for the first time this evening, she is scared. Then the downstairs steel door clangs open. She freezes.

"What you doin' up there?" a man yells. "Come down!"

A weak glow appears below her.

"Get down here, bitch!"

The glow gets brighter.

"Things be bad for you if you make me come get you."

Shit. What a time to be without a heater.

The glow grows — Clare guesses that he's leaning into the stairwell, shining his lantern up to the first landing. Now there's a slight earthy smell. The heat of compost batteries — hot cowshit (more or less). The guard must have a flashlight, and Clare is excited. This is electric light — or the closest thing we'll ever see in our lifetimes. Then the smell and glare get stronger and brighter.

He's creeping up the stairs. She turns and climbs too, stopping every ten steps to listen.

Nothing.

Then the glow turns to a clear sheet of light below her. She's only about a flight and a half ahead of him. Clare hurries up the steps as quietly as she can. *What floor am I on?* She's lost count. She thinks that this is seven. The nanny tries the door, but her key doesn't work. She tries the lock on the next floor; that door stays locked as well. Clare has overshot her floor. This must be nine or ten. She starts to shake her head in panic. *I can't backtrack — the guard is too close.* What to do but continue higher? She goes up four more floors. Things stay dark. She pauses to listen. Her heart bashing in her chest. Silence in the stairwell. The compost smell is stronger, but maybe it's just the updraft. Watching the dark is incredibly unnerving, especially when her vision is full of iridescent water spots.

She turns and just rushes up the steps. In New York City, only the first twelve floors of any building are occupied. I've heard that on the West Coast fire marshals only allow tenants to live on the first three floors — while down in Dallas, cowboys roam freely from the basements to the roofs on any Lone Star skyscraper. But Clare is no Texan and all this stair-climbing has made her start panting. She is sure that she must be up to the fifteenth by now.

The dark is really grinding her up. The nanny's cheeks and nose are numb. Bob Dylan's "Ghost of Electricity" howls from the bones of this nanny's face. She begins whispering, "Drugs. Drugs. Drugs. I want my drugs." Clare is suddenly sure that she would rather go blind than be in this dark any longer — that is, assuming the blind see true nothingness, not amorphous spots of texture. She wonders if she's really in this stairwell or having a DT coma. She stops climbing, allows herself the luxury of memory —

there was a winter in Nagasaki when she watched a blind man skate. She was just a girl. The juice hadn't disappeared yet in Japan — she and the blind man were the only skaters using this indoor rink. At first, Clare didn't know the skater was blind — he was wearing *Blues Brothers* Wayfarers and a kind of fool's skullcap. She named him Mr. Shades as he began skating a leisurely circle, staying close to the railing. There was nothing hesitant about his slow speed. He looked like he knew what he was doing. She stood and watched him skate closer toward her. She realized that if she didn't move, he would plow right into her.

He's playing chicken with me!

Clare held her ground — she wasn't going to back down. His skates made scar-sounds on the ice. Mr. Shades skated right up to the girl, but swerved at the last moment. His mouth was without expression. He made another leisurely circuit. Clare didn't move. Once again, the man swerved at the last minute. After several more rotations and swerve-dodges, Clare got bored and raced to the center of the ice, intending to spin some mad show-off pirouettes, but crashed into the skating man.

"Shit to this!" he yelled in Japanese as he thumped on his ass, his sunglasses clattering across the ice. Clare landed next to him, more embarrassed than hurt. She looked and saw he was indeed Asian. He started frantically patting the ice. She didn't get it. "Please," he said in Japanese, "where are my glasses?"

He stared at her — but *staring* wasn't what he was doing. He had eyes, but they were just a smear of milky blue. She had never seen a blind Asian before. It terrified her. She scrambled up and quickly skated away — all the while, the man crying, "Please. Please. Where are my glasses?"

· · ·

There's always a moment when Clare tells this story to one of her "paramours" for the first time. "Why didn't I pick up that poor man's glasses?" she'll ask rhetorically. "For twenty years I've felt terrible about it. I use this memory to understand what regret is." Sometimes she ends the story this way: "I'm convinced that I'll be remembering his, 'Please. Please. Where are my glasses?' when I'm on my deathbed." Clare never mentions this prediction if she and the guy are in a bed. But why not? If a woman ever told me that in bed . . . in fact, if Clare and I were in bed together — what a thought! (With all this sheldraking, this is the first I've constructed that scenario.) . . . Anyway, if we were in bed together and she said those words, I'd smile at the irony. Then quote some interesting deathbed-speak — appropriate to quote to you all now because these are the last words of Raymond Hood, the main architect of Radio City itself. I wasn't there, mind you — he died half a century before I was born. My third wife (the woman of prominent cheekbones and narrow chin), Allissa Sontag, came across Hood's quote and found it inspiring: "A beautiful woman's beauty is in proportion to her utility." Oh, did Allissa get hot to write a biography of a man who built skyscrapers as utilitarian monuments to womanhood. Then she discovered that he repudiated his earlier statement. On his deathbed.

I have no idea if Hood saw a vision of Muybridge horses before he took the big sleep, but the man looked up from the pillow and his last words were, "This beauty stuff is all bunk."

This beauty stuff is all bunk? If I said this to Clare, she would probably say, "There's certainly no beauty in blindness." Then

she'd make two fists and say, "Now, let me tell you about death-
beds. Let me tell you about Vengeance withdrawal."

Clare turns around. There's no narcotic at the end of this
stairwell. *I'm going back down. I need my drugs.* If she runs into
the guard, she'll just talk her way out of any trouble, assuming he
is foolish enough to still be stumbling around in this dark.

After an hour of careful stepping and trying of doors, Clare
reaches the bottom of the stairs. Then she turns and carefully
counts her way back up to the seventh floor. She feels her keys.
Without warning, a sharp cone of light spills beside her. Clare
shocks up with fear. But she's also excited. Electricity is thrilling —
the best narcotic of all! She squeezes the wingtips between her
knees as she scrunches against the wall. Now the guard comes
down the stairs. His flashlight is small and he's training the light
at his feet. He's looking for something? As the man passes, Clare
has the crazy impulse to drop to her knees and stick out her tongue
in that light — *just to taste those hot photons, oh!*

But she doesn't. She holds her breath. The guard doesn't see
her, but he doesn't continue to the next floor — he unlocks the
door to Clare's office and steps in. The stairs are now full of a great
earthy smell — the hot stink of electric light. Clare starts to cry.
She's only seen electric light three times in the past ten years, and
each time, the beauty of it floored her. But she never cried. Until
now. Then she knows: *These tears are for the blind skater.* After
twenty years, Clare can finally cry for him. Not because she didn't
give him his sunglasses. The nanny is crying because the Japanese
skater will never see the joyful leap of light. The nanny wonders
if these tears have transcended her need for a Vengeance fix.

No. Probably not.

Although I say her thoughts have redeemed Raymond Hood
in the belly of the General Electric Building. Surely the architect's

lonely ghost now sees that beauty is light. And light is only bunk to a blind man.

Now Clare hears voices. From behind the door. A woman's Irish lilt. Kathleen Keegan. What's she doing here so late? Clare presses her ear to the door — but all she hears is muffled syllables. Ghosts of talk. Then she clearly hears Keegan's laugh. "Mrs. Eddy says, 'Angels are pure thoughts from God, winged with Truth and Love, no matter what their individualism may be.'"

Suddenly a man says, "And a martini is a pure thought from you."

"So shall my mind be astir?" Keegan says playfully.

"Hell, no." The man laughs. "Shake that sucker good."

Now a shaking noise. Bones in tin — a cocktail shaker. Clare knows enough about the Science of Liquor to guess that this repartee has something to do with martini commandment *Shaken, not stirred*. Every nanny knows that Kathleen Keegan started her career pouring liquor for Americans in the days of Reagan and electricity, Keegan's uncle having coaxed her to leave Ireland to come tend his bar in New York. And she did, sloshing suds at the Lost Weekend, an upscale pseudo-dive in the West Village. A year later she was forced to change professions when a cousin back home scored a stateside job as an *Irish Echo* nanny and stepped off the plane trying to hide her own big belly with her suitcase. "The girl had a contract to care for some upscaler's newborn," Keegan told Clare on more than one occasion. "My uncle made me take her place." The old woman always shrugged. "I protested plenty, but a girl like me ends up either pouring a man's beer or raising his children. What's the difference?"

. . .

Not much, apparently, Clare thinks. *I thought I was the boss's protégé, but I don't know the old lady at all.* It's outrageous enough to think Keegan is a secret junkie popping sugar cubes, but the night bartender for the guards at Radio City as well? Or maybe there is an actual heavenly visitor in there. . . .

Footsteps come toward the door. "Thirsty angel thanks you," a man's voice says. "Tomorrow, then."

Without thinking, Clare races down the stairs ahead of the guard or angel. In the lobby, she hears the gramophone still spinning and panics. *How am I going to get my drugs now?*

She hurries out into the night where it's dark, but at least there are gaslights. Clare walks through the orange and green glow shaking her head. Suddenly she leans over and shudders and gets sick. In the gaslight glow above the crown of her head I clearly see the horses again. I see the rider with the sickle. Clare looks up and squints. My God, does she see them too?

"Vengeance is mine sayeth the Lord," a man calls from the shadows.

Clare looks around. Spies a figure in the shadows. Her dealer. The nanny starts crying in gratitude. "Oh man. Oh man, if you only knew what I've been through searching for you."

Fifty bucks and one glassine envelope later, Clare crouches in the shadow of a Dumpster and mainlines the Vengeance in her neck like the oldtime thrash-junkies in Seattle used to do. I'm embarrassed that I witnessed this. I know Clare herself hates being this crude, but it's the best way to get an immediate rush. As the dope hits, Clare tilts back her head and smiles. Nothing crude about the joy on her face. I look at her eyes. What if we imagine Clare and a more conventional belle presented before us, both with their eyes closed. Say, Clare with Louise Brooks. Now consider Louise's lovely face. No wonder Bob Dylan wrote "Seems Like a Freeze Out" (a.k.a. "Visions of Joanna") after viewing Louise holding a handful of rain up on the screen at the Bleecker Street Cinema. But watch both women open their eyes. See the metamorphosis in Clare's face! Her simultaneously daffy-tragic gaze positively infuses the nanny with an anxious beauty. Louise Brooks just looks awake.

This is what's going through my mind. As to what's going through Clare's — it's an hour before dawn and Manhattan has never seemed brighter. The nanny almost feels compelled to sing a little ode of joy to the gaslights. She's heard that in the old plug-and-light-switch days, men and women would even read the *New York Times* by streetlight. She hurries west toward the downtown trolley stop, trying to imagine electric streetlights. The citizens must have danced around each lamppost like revelers around a Maypole, the women not bothering to hide their multiple orgasms. Then Clare remembers what her dad said. No orgasms. Instead, women stood under pools of light reading the Sunday *New York Times* Style section.

Not that she could read *Style section* in any case.

But I could.

Yes! Me. Dylan. I can tell her this because I am, in fact, no longer merely sheldraking her in a Times Square nickelodeon, but following the woman on Forty-ninth Street. And I yell out, "Clare! Clare, stop!"

She whips around, gesturing for her gun. Lucky for me, she

isn't armed. I understand how reasonable her search is. Imagine you're walking outside of Radio City at four in the morning and a strange man yells, "Ishmael!

"Ishmael!

"Ish!"

You'd reach for your gun too. Clare realizes she is Glockless, so she leans into a garbage can. What? Then she shoots up holding a black club. It's shaped like a bowling pin. What gives? In the gaslight, I see a crinkled reflection — tinfoil. It's a black champagne bottle. Who tossed it? What's there to celebrate? Intuitively, I decide that it's empty. And I get to experience the bottle's empty state firsthand right after Clare takes three leaping steps and hits my shoulder with it.

At the moment of impact, I realize what's happening to me. Yes. I'm being hit with a bottle. But in the bigger picture, I figure out what happened to me when I first glimpsed Clare in Washington Square Park.

Love.

Oh that lost word. Wait. Dig this Hallmark Greeting Card phrase, Hollywood phrase, Harlequin Romance phrase: *Love at first sight.*

Who among us has taken this fall since the wattage left so long ago? Look Ishmaels, I'll state what no one over forty ever admits: We never fall head over heels in love anymore. The only relationships of substance are those formed before electricity disappeared. Say like that editor and his wife in Washington Square Park. Like the two seafaring babynappers. Sure the rest of us meet and couple. Date. Roll in the hay. Try to mate. Even the most jaded guy-on-the-street is capable of companioning up. But no one has experienced love's rapture and heartache, let alone simple infatuation, since the Millennium. If my father were still alive he'd just say we were all wearing god-ugly Schopenhauer duck pants. Electric-age doctors used to name this state *hypopituitarism*. Translation: Your glands aren't working.

Ha!

When Con Ed died, the docs clammed up and just watched us all "hypopit" out. Watched us all experience a brownout of the heart. Everyone just goes through the motions of romance. That's why I've been married so many times. Clare is so unsure of amour, she covets her beloved's shoes. And through our hollow examples, Ishmaels like you go through the motions of amour as well. Remember all the boys that you told your mothers that you loved? Your mothers knew in their hearts, but could never admit to you, that you had no idea what you were talking about. If love is food, you were exalting the Big Mac without ever having eaten T-bone in Texas. Or in vegetarian-speak, you wept tears of joy over iceberg lettuce without experiencing the hot bite of arugula.

I know I'm talking foolishness. But foolish is how I feel. A horse's ass. My God, I just fell for Clare. Something a man used to be able to do without sheldraking. Something a guy did without worrying it would kill him. Wait. He knew it would kill him and that's what made it delicious: *I'll die of this love.* Ha! The last man to die for love was John Barrymore. The last woman, Greta Garbo. And that happened in the silent days, before talkies. Decades before electricity vanished.

If this sounds foolish, I remind you I'm a guy who's been hit with a champagne bottle. When Clare clouts my shoulder again — (if I were a baseball pitcher it would be, "Good-bye, World Series") — the bottle bangs my ear on the upswing. And fuck love-at-first-sight. I yell that F-word, then start shouting, "Lindy! Lindy! Lindy!"

As I roll and hug my shoulder, I realize that the part of my consciousness that swims far above my bodily and romantic concerns has just reasoned that shouting *Lindy!* is the only way to stop Clare from beating me to death. And I do get her attention. She stands above me, asking, "What did you say?" I make to get up, but she wobbles the bottle at me — "Stay."

Huh? Am I a dog?

"Lindy." I pant.

"Lindy what?"

I catch my breath and say, "I am the Lindys' son."

I am lying.

"You're Soda's father?" Clare asks, her voice squeaking upward like a hiccup. For some reason, I assume she's jabbering about soda (small S) and I say, "No, no. I'm not thirsty."

Then I get it. She assumes the old Lindys are really the baby's grandparents. I kneel.

"No!" she commands. "Stay down."

I ignore her and start to stand. Clare reaches to help — then remembers the true Valkyrie response to this scene . . . and bashes my shoulder again with the bottle.

Oh, what an effective club!

Now I am rolling and low-trash swearing at Clare — to hell with shouting *Lindy! Lindy!* I'm in love with this woman, but I slang her out with the street term designating every girl's locus. I'm well aware the Vengeance jungle drums are beating in her head, but instead of clubbing me to death, she turns and runs away.

This is wrong, she's thinking. *He wasn't stealing a baby.*

She has to be by herself and sort out her Vengeance.

4 ballad of a thin man

LET'S SAY Clare paces Twenty-third Street until the Chelsea dawn. Then she ferries across the Hudson. On the deck of the boat she has this crazy thought about the wingtips she's wearing — *These shoes are what walked me into trouble.* In fact, *This footwear is evil.*

Of course! Paramour #3 was a trust fund brat who wore the Devil's shoes. She slides them off. Jiggles both shoes in her hands as if she's judging their weight. Then, one by one, Clare throws the shoes overboard. Hears them give two splashes slight as leaping fish.

Then she wiggles her bare feet. *What should a shoeless girl do now?*

The ferry docks and Clare heads to the Reagan Mon, where all the barefoot girls slide over on the Hoop to make room. *At last, I've revealed myself to be one of them. Ha!* The girls clear a much bigger space than Clare needs, which is surprising because newcomers usually get crowded ass-to-ass. The generosity of these barefoot sitters makes Clare feel guilty about her intentions. She ignores the zone they've created and circles the Hoop checking out the shoes. *Ah ha!* There's a pair of flimsy slingbacks that look like they'll fit. Clare squeezes between two girls, and after she is settled, everyone returns to shuffling their bare feet on the ground thigh-to-thigh.

Clare fakes the drill too: She sits — eyes closed — rubbing her bare feet against the cold ground. She can actually feel the girls' collective contemplation of fertility. Not that she has any interest in achieving that state. Clare senses the energy surging through the marble she's sitting on. Her legs are tingling. It's as if gravity itself is surging upward from the ground. Clare imagines that her womb is now going on-line. *Christ! Cone Heart was bad enough — all I need now is to get spontaneously pregnant.* She stands and then stoops quickly to steal her Hoop partner's slingbacks. The owner is too busy rubbing her feet, willing up fertility, to notice the theft, and Clare hurries across the grass. As Clare runs, she does feel remorse. Kinda. She just needed some shoes. Suddenly, Clare steps into a clump of dogshit. "Okay. This is my punishment. My slate is clear."

She walks for several blocks, searching for a garden hose or puddle, but ends up just wiping her feet over and over on someone's lawn, a chlorophyll wash. Then she puts the shoes on.

Prissy, she thinks. *Definitely non-Lit footwear.*

When the nanny finally ends up at Big Pink, Mr. Lindy opens the front door — "Clare, there you are!" — the concern in his voice disconcerting somehow.

"I didn't want to just barge in because I'm so late," Clare says.

"You don't look well!" he says. "Are you okay?"

Clare hears Mrs. Lindy singing *fa-fa-fa*. Then start singing that damn familiar song.

"Clare, are you sure you're okay?" Mr. Lindy is asking.

"Oh, yes," she sighs and lies. "The neighbors were banging around again last night, and I didn't get any sleep. I just need a bucket of coffee."

He nods. "Oh, I know about neighbors. . . ."

On cue, there is a crash upstairs and something metallic rolls the length of the floor. Both Clare and Mr. Lindy watch the ceiling until the noise stops. Then they look at each other.

Clare speaks first. "I'll go check on Soda."

She looks into the crib — the baby's arms wave madly, as if directing things to roll across the upstairs floor. The child now gazes warmly up at Clare.

"Oh, widdel baby woo," Clare baby-talks. "Drop dead, fuck you."

The nanny grits her teeth. She's mainlined Vengeance. No Cone Heart can penetrate her now. She turns from the crib and starts shaking — a junkie nanny too strung to even worry about Cone Heart. Too tired to wonder how Soda fits into the parade of Lindy baby mobiles. Clare doesn't even wonder about me. But she should — her lovesick fool is sailing for Jersey at this very moment.

Clare pinches the baby on the hip. Soda scowls, but doesn't cry. In fact, the child glances at Clare with complete disinterest.

Poolhall Baby — guys cultivate this look in between shots. Clare frowns. She has seen Soda act remote before — but remote the way car alarms were once remote. This is different. The baby is acting apathetic.

Apathy is a state babies never enter.

Clare looks away. *This little shit-sack baby is creeping me out. I gotta get out of here for a moment.* She heads for the door. *I'm going on a milk run.* She'll risk going out without an umbrella. But she won't chance these shoes, slips on a pair of Mrs. Lindy's flats. This is a wise choice, because down at the Reagan Mon, a barefoot girl is searching the grass. When Clare arrives, the girl almost points — *That's the bitch who took my shoes!* Then the barefoot girl notes that this bitch isn't wearing slingbacks. Nevertheless, the barefoot girl tails Clare, unsure what to do. Then a man steps from the trees — his coat over his head like an umbrella — and calls to the shoe thief, "Clare! Clare!"

It's me.

And I'm now blocking the barefoot girl. Clare turns. I point to a birch — *oooh, my shoulder still smarts* — and say, "Alexander Hamilton was shot under this tree."

This is all that I know about this portion of Jersey (it may very well be all that I know of the Garden State — not that any woman has ever tested me). The barefoot girl glances at the tree and doesn't know what to do. Now that I am here, she is outnumbered. She begins to doubt her initial impression — maybe Clare is not the thief. The barefoot girl shuffles away, halfhearted.

Clare had been aware of this girl all along and is actually relieved that I've appeared. But who am I? Clare doesn't ask. She just demands, "Who's Alexander Hamilton?"

"You've never heard of him?"

"Was he some Jersey mobster?"

"No, he's the guy who claimed Thomas Edison stole his patent for the lightbulb," I explain. "So he challenged the inventor to a duel." I point to a space between the trees. "They both faced each other right over there with their pistols and lightbulbs."

I'm making most of this up — but all women are charmed by stories about the Electric Days. And I'm trying my damnedest to be charming. Clare looks where I'm pointing and asks, "What kind of pistols?"

Jesus Christ, nannies and their firearms! Who cares? Clare starts to walk away.

"They were using some sort of antique flintlock pistols," I call out. "The two men faced each other, each with a gun in his right hand and a single lightbulb in his left. Thomas E. fired first and gave Hamilton a third eye." Clare looks back at me. "Yes, literally! It was a weird kind of bullet. A round ball. Hamilton actually plucked it out of his forehead." I demonstrate. "He held it in his palm and examined it. Then he fell to the grass dead."

Clare gives me a brief smile, then continues to the milk wagon, saying, "Should I be afraid of you or what?"

She says this assuming that I'm tagging along behind her.

Which after a moment's consideration I am — I'm just a victim of magnetic attraction.

"Look," I say. "I am just a man trying to find my parents — my true parents if they are still alive."

This is a lie. And I'm telling it to the back of her head. "The man I thought was my father died when I was a boy, and before Mom died two months later she told me I was adopted."

Again, I'm lying.

But only to Clare — I've never lied to you. What I said about my Lit Wear lineage is true. I'll eventually reveal my real intentions to Clare, and just before I do, I'll alert you. But for now, consider the lie I'm spinning. You're all Modern Girls, and I'm wondering if you can imagine the ensuing scene, because Clare is a Modern Girl too — and she can't. She can't picture my mother propped on her deathbed, saying: "Dylan, I've kept this secret all these years and I gotta tell ya before I go . . . I have always been the mother of Dylan . . . but I didn't bear ya. You was born to another woman."

"You mean I was adopted?" I ask.

She coughs. Drops her head back. "Yes. Yes."

Then she dies.

Consider that scenario. Can you see my mother on her pillows? Can you see the little boy's expression as he says, "You mean I was adopted?" I ask because Clare can't see it — she wants more details: What kind of bed? Did it have sheets? What time of day was it? She's not asking these questions because I'm a bad actor. Clare just has zero visual imagination. She didn't grow up with Hollywood current, thus her cerebral cortex is as underdeveloped as an agrarian Third World country. And I must spin out this elaborate lie: I'm an orphan searching for my true parents. And I've traced hundreds of records. And I now think my real parents are the Lindys.

I feel guiltless lying to Clare — lovers live for fabrication — but I know it is wrong to put my real father's last words into the lips of a fictitious mother. Dad was the one who had been lying under a soft pile of Melvilles — cuddling his fabric like a baby — when he looked up and said, "Son, it's starting to rain. . . ."

Then he was gone.

I tell Clare that my mother told me about the rain after she

announced that I was an orphan. Then she unconsciously para-
phrased Raymond Hood, whispering, "Beauty is bunk." And died.
The beauty remark goes right by Clare. But she has already bitten
on my mom's supposed rain comment and now considers that my
story might be true.

I walk Clare back to Big Pink — doing sideways alligator-eyes,
checking her out. Her posture is perfect, Clare's head so erect it's
as if she's balancing books on her crown. She has elongated the
very scaffolding of both her nape and throat. Ah, her voice box
moves. She speaks. "There's your possible mother."

I face forward — we're walking in the same direction as an
old woman pushing a baby carriage a block ahead.

"That's Mrs. Lindy," Clare says. "Let's catch up. I'll intro-
duce you?"

I shake my head.

"Why not?"

Damn! I won't confess my lie. "I'm not prepared to meet the
woman," I start to say. God, that sounds lame. But Clare is no
longer interested in me or my search — the girl with no shoes has
suddenly zigzagged off a lawn and cut between us and Mrs. Lindy.
To my eyes it looks as if the girl is stalking the baby carriage. *What,
you think the baby has your slingbacks?*

Clare emits a profanity in a husky voice.

Me: "What's wrong?"

Dumb question.

The barefoot girl quickens her pace to a trot and swoops by
Mrs. Lindy. It's not slingbacks she's after — she's scooping the
baby out of the carriage.

"Soda!" Clare yells.

The barefoot girl hugs the child to her chest and tears across the street. Mrs. Lindy stands frozen for a moment, then chases after her. I turn to Clare — she's patting herself under her arms. I have a flashback of one of my wives making this same gesture when she powdered after a shower. For the second time today, Clare is making this useless gesture, looking for her Glock, her absent Model 30 left back in Alphabet City.

The unarmed nanny barks a word that sounds like *ihayaka!* — then takes off running. I now see the old mother on her hands and knees on a front lawn. Several Japanese women run off the porch of Big Pink, shouting, "Mrs. Lindy! Mrs. Lindy!"

But the meno-mother just swats the air with a single arm, gasping, "I'm just winded. I'm just winded." As Clare reaches the lawn, the old woman points toward a backyard. Clare doesn't break stride — she just tears into the yard, her running reminding me of women tearing across stage at Lucinda Childs revivals at Carnegie Hall, marimba/xylophones doing fake-electro Philip Glass doo-dahs while the dancers exaggerate their hips and leap, turning themselves into women of pure limb and reach.

This is what I'm thinking as I watch Clare disappear. Then I start running myself, heading down the block, paralleling Clare, intending to cut the babynapper off at the pass. I run between a pair of Jersey colonials. Now the backyard, suburban topography. Here's an abandoned barbecue grill. Plastic doodad toys lying inside a wet sandbox. Now, an aluminum rowboat on cinder blocks. Lines of upside-down pants gliding between the houses — both Jersey Americans and Asian-borns hoisting in their laundry before the peak birding hours start.

Now I see the barefoot girl. She's heading my way, hugging the baby as if she's trying to thrust the kid inside her chest, her teeth clenched in a grimace at the effort. In her exertion, the girl's jaw and teeth almost look as if they've transformed into extensions of her shoulders, her mouth now a double row of molars. Thick cow teeth. I run to block Ms. Cow Mouth. I'm moving in a crouch, my arms open. Football players monkey around this way, but I haven't done this since I was a kid. What a moment to feel nostalgia . . . But wait! An abrupt line of black kimonos shoots across my horizon. A laundry line! A curtain of black hiding the kidnapper. I see her bare feet on the grass beneath the kimonos. Then the woman barrels through the Japanese laundry clutching her bundle. I'm about to tackle her, but hesitate. *Don't hurt the baby.* I grab the woman's waist with one arm — but her right arm whips out from under the baby, a black sap in her fist — *swear to God!* It looks like a bread stick made of charcoal. I know that it feels like lead when it strikes you. I've pissed off a few bouncers in my time and know a man doesn't want to get whacked on the head with such a sap any more than he wants a champagne clubbing. I hold my free arm above my head as a shield. She plows forward and I go with the weight and my arm gets tangled in a damn clothesline. Ms. Cow Mouth smashes the sap on the delicate point of my elbow.

The chord of pain that shoots up my arm makes me collapse on the grass. I'm rolling down on the lawn, gripping the crook of my arm, sweat drenching my face as I make raspy mewing sounds, too shocked for even yelling.

A hand on my shoulder. I look up — Clare's face encompasses the sky. "You okay?"

I nod.

"Good," she says remotely and touches my head. I intuit this was a professional gesture. That I'm a fellow nanny now. Where's my toot of Vengeance?

I stagger up from the grass, cupping my elbow. Both women are gone. I begin tearing through these bleak backyards in the direction of the ferry — I can at least make sure the barefoot babynapper doesn't escape by water. I rush down a steep walkway to the terminal and realize that I'm listening for gunshots.

But Clare is not armed, you say.

Wrong. I always know when a woman has found herself a gun — the Morphic Resonance of that weapon shimmering stronger through the air than a simple intuition. I sheldrake the gun in Clare's hand.

This gun is not confirmed immediately. All afternoon, I cool my heels beneath the Reagan Mon — within sight of the ferry — on the lookout for Clare or kidnapper. Then a voice is behind me, laughing. "Hey big boy, share some dope about Thomas Edison?"

Some scout I am. I turn. "Are you okay, Clare?"

The nanny nods.

"And the baby?"

"The little shit is fine," she says, touching my forearm. "How's your elbow?"

"Okay."

What she says next surprises me: "Let's scram."

"Wait. What happened?"

"I'll tell you on the ferry." She walks toward the terminal. What choice do I have? I follow. Clare isn't moving like an assassin — maybe she didn't actually shoot the barefoot girl. We both board the boat in silence and end up getting sandwiched between troops of Drexels.

I continue to say nothing.

The sails are hoisted — I'm silent.

"All right," Clare finally says. "I ran and caught her." She glances at her feet. "These flats are miserable to run in." She glances at my cowboy boots. "Nice."

I lift my cuffs and she admires the boots' stitching. Then Clare looks up at my face and says, "I ran through every backyard looking for that bitch. I was sure I'd lost her and lost Soda. I started to hyperventilate — Kathleen Keegan says this is just mock-mother panic that nannies get when they lose their wards. But I've never lost a baby before. It was my *heart* I was feeling —" Clare touches her forehead when she says the H-word, but doesn't elaborate. She's not going to confess Cone Heart. "I had to lean against a pole and do some of Kathleen Keegan's breathing exercises before I fainted or worse. Then I looked up. I was standing below a bird-house, and some twenty-odd birds were examining me, each one sticking its head out an opening. This was one of those post of-fices — those neo-pigeons each expecting me to give them mes-sages to deliver. Then I sensed someone was standing in front of me. I turned and saw her — a strange woman had crept up. What an amazing stiff fräulein. She was so soft of foot she had to be a professional. Without saying a word she held out this exquisite Browning."

I frown. "You needed a scarf?"

Clare rolls her eyes. "Not Lit Wear, dummy." She says *dummy* playfully. "A revolver. The Browning is the most beautiful handgun ever tooled." She shakes her head. "Amateurs . . ."

I shrug.

"Anyway, this nanny wasn't from the Nanny Broker Com-pany, but I still took the piece," Clare says. "The moment I touched the barrel the birdhouse above me exploded into motion. We both looked up to see this stream of neo-pigeons flocking out of the structure. What was this — a fraternity birdhouse? The sky

became solid birds, and the woman said, 'I hate this mystic shit —
but you should follow them.' The birds were flying east to the
city, which is the direction I headed. I hate that 'mystic shit' too —
but you and I both followed the same tactic — I wanted to make
sure the barefoot kidnapper didn't float with Soda back to Manhattan. There's a stone stairway that cuts down the hill to the ferry
terminal. I started racing down the steps, and at the first landing
there she was. I almost ran right past her. The barefoot girl. She
was just leaning against the railing, cradling Soda."

Clare stops talking and tugs inside the blouse of her Far from
the Madding Crowd — she's trying to pull something out, but
gets a ring snagged on her bra strap. I gingerly reach over to untan-
gle her finger. My touch is particularly gentle as I loop the delicate
white strap. My fingertip touches the flesh of her shoulder. Clare's
hand is now free and she pulls a monstrous revolver from under
her blouse. I'm still touching her shoulder. She throws the heater
into the Hudson. I'm still touching her shoulder. The gun falls
slow. Slo mo. The gun falls slower than a baby. Slower than a
man's shoe. Somehow my hands have ended up in front of me —
clasped together like those of a minister. The gun splashes. I know
that I've gone on about sheldraking, but I'm not into New Age
mystic shit any more than Clare is. Then a conviction comes to
me and I find myself saying, "If anyone is throwing the I-Ching
at this moment, they'll get the Joyous River hexagram."

Clare looks at me. Then she shakes her head. "No. They will
get, *The superior woman decides lawsuits / And carries out punishment.*"

She leans against the railing.

"Was it that bad?" I ask her, glancing at this superior woman's
clothes for splattering of blood.

"No. It wasn't bad at all," Clare says. "There was no gunplay. I just took little Soda from the girl."

"You didn't shoot her?"

Clare shakes her head.

"Why the mercy?" I look at Clare's hands again.

"Those Yakuza-nanny rumors are lies." She wrinkles her nose.

I am confused. "What rumors?"

"You know how Yakuzas — real ones, real Japanese gangsters — are required to cut off a finger if they screw up or lose their nerve?"

I lift my arms, showing empty hands. "I have no firsthand experience."

"Well, nannies are not bound by the same code — we don't lose a finger every time we screw up."

"Oh." I don't believe her.

She starts to say something else. Then she doesn't. Then she speaks the words. "Cone Heart." She pauses. "I didn't shoot the barefoot girl because of Cone Heart."

She doesn't say any more. But I know about Cone Heart. I can imagine Soda fixing Clare with The Gaze. Enraptured, the nanny lowers her weapon unfired.

"Okay. Okay. The rumors are true," Clare finally says. "My marksmanship teacher only has four fingers on each hand. Women like that just wear special gloves with false fingers."

"I won't tell," I say, taking her hand. I'm using a serious tone — no one is going to cut anyone's fingers . . .

"Why didn't you go meet Mrs. Lindy?" Clare suddenly asks, scowling a bit.

I shrug. "Let's talk about it later."

She smiles, slurs, "Whenz later?"

"Over dinner."

"Huh? This a date?"

I look shocked. "Of course not. Let's just be civilized."

"Oh. You're one of those men who are into civilization — God, I should never have tossed the Browning."

We disembark at Fourteenth Street and I ask her, "So when you're carrying a gun, does that mean a civilized man shouldn't get closer than half a mile?"

"No. I like my civilization within gun range."

I'm getting embarrassed reporting our repartee. I assure you that I'm not deliberately trying to do an electric days—*Thin Man* number with this woman. I steer Clare/Myrna Loy toward restaurant-cum-clubs with roped-off entrances. Wait. I'm lying again. I'm metaphorically *working the stage* here. I'm *working* this girl. But why not? In the electric days, when a guy fell for a girl, he didn't worry at first whether she was falling for him. Wait. Now I get it. We New Yorkers, maybe all of Western Civilization, have forgotten so much about romance since volts took a powder that we're functional idiots. It's been so long since I've fallen for a girl that I forgot about a psychic state called *mutual attraction*. Not that a guy thought about that state in the electric era. Guys were so optimistic back then they assumed if they asked a girl to Nell's on Fourteenth Street, she'd say, "Sure. What time?"

And Nell's is where I steer her — it's got the biggest crowd outside the door. The bouncers are choosing the diners who'll be allowed in (ah, surely a black sap in each jacket), and as newcomers, we are forced to the front of the line. But Clare works us to the rear in less than five minutes. She's good. I've never seen a girl better at avoiding the bouncer's glance. We stand without speaking for a while. Then Clare leans close. "In the old days, the object was to be so cool you didn't have to wait, right?"

I smile. "How old are the days to which you refer?"

"When you were a young gadfly."

"No. Those were the home-cooked-meal days. My father's days are the ones you mean. I remember Dad telling me how he was waved into Nell's before Keith Richards."

I suddenly catch myself. *Shit!* Would an orphan call his adoptive father *Dad?*

"I don't think I'll ever stop thinking of him as my father," I say.

"Huh?" Clare says. She wasn't even listening. I try to change the subject, but then it doesn't seem possible that my subterfuge can last another moment: Here on Fourteenth Street, my mother — the very woman who spent fifty-seven hours and thirty-nine minutes in labor giving birth to yours truly — totters out of Nell's. She's short, plump, and exquisitely dressed. With her crew-cut, she has butch Twentieth Century Gertrude Stein dignity. She stomps away, but damn! if her radar doesn't pick up her one-and-only. She turns and tilts her head up. "Oh, Dylan! What are *you* doing here?" She says this as if Nell's is too good for me. For twenty years Mother has tried to score one of the two dozen real penthouses left in the city — each, of course, in a building with twelve stories or less. And for twenty years every coop board from Gramercy Park to Turtle Bay has turned her down because I am not a fashionable son to have as an associate. She now peers at Clare and registers that I am robbing the cradle, although not scandalously (I remind you that Mom and I both do youth drugs — separately! — her doing a hefty bong full of Teen Spirit now and then). I can tell that the woman is on nothing at the present, and she extends her right hand. Clare reaches out to shake, but my mother turns her wrist, offering her knuckles. She expects to be kissed? Oh damn, she's been hanging out with that Windsor crowd again. "I'm Dylan's mother," she announces.

This is the moment that the bouncer chooses to signal me with a slight wave of his own hand. He likes the look of me (or more likely, Clare), because he makes this motion subtly, giving us the option to edge backward through the line and pretend that we didn't see. But, status be damned — I nod at the bouncer. He looks disappointed, but unhooks the velvet rope. As I guide Clare forward, she pats my mom's knuckles, then stuffs what appears to be a fresh Kleenex into the old woman's hand, saying, "Here."

We almost make it to the door when a lightbulb appears above Clare's head — a metaphoric one, that is (I'm not hallucinating the *Christ as Electrician* poster, lightbulb over his halo). I refer to comic strips of the old kilowatt days. Whenever a character got an idea, the artists would draw a shining lightbulb above Charlie Brown or Mickey M. The nanny's lightbulb is this: *The woman this man just described lying on her deathbed saying, "Son, it's raining," is very much alive.* Clare now raises her hand to her mouth (her lips an *oh*).

"I'm out of here," she says and rushes back into the line — "Hey!" "Watch it!" "Bitch!" Mom gives me a theatrical shrug. I follow Clare, trying to get her to stop.

Why did I throw away that Browning? Clare is surely thinking as she just starts running down the sidewalk. I find myself chasing after. *This is all wrong,* I'm thinking.

In those long-ago ampere days, men might fiddle with shortwave radios and do wiretaps, but they didn't need to chase their beloved down the street in front of their own mothers. But I don't want to lose this woman. And Clare has never run from anything in her life — nannies aren't chicken. She must be literally running from love!

The odds of this may be iffy, but I don't care. She's tearing across Fourteenth Street — and me too. She heads up Fifth. I follow. Now I'm a man who has chased a woman or two in my time, but my quarry always wore *Joan Crawford fuck-me's,* ridiculous shoes with awkward stalks — murder to dance in, only good for a kick, much too expensive to abandon. As for Clare, her flats make a slapping sound on the pavement. Then this running woman pauses a beat and kicks her right shoe off — a low kick, the flat landing in the gutter. Then Clare takes another step and it's as if she is consumed by the true science of kicking, because with this left kick her ankle reaches the height of her shoulders. This second shoe really sails! It arcs over a gaslight. Wow! The ghosts of Rockettes gnash their teeth with envy! Now Clare is running barefoot up Fifth Avenue. Her bare feet and ankles are beautiful to watch. I think that I'm actually slowing down to prolong our run and watch the motion of her hips under her Far from the Madding Crowd. Then suddenly Clare screams and tumbles to the pavement.

She gives a brief holler.

Rolls and leans against the window of a lantern-lit bodega.

I run over.

She raises her fists. "Fuck it! You got no gun. I got no gun. But I'll kill you with my bare hands."

I hold my hands up even with my shoulders in the universal "I'm harmless" position. "Hold it. Hold it," I say. "I'm cool."

I then see a little glass shark fin embedded in her arch. "Shit. I'll help."

I hurry inside the store and buy the first sensible thing I see — a quart of Perrier. I run back to Clare — the blood is really flowing — and kneel down beside her.

"I'll take it out," I say.

She swats my hand and slides the glass out herself, quickly squeezing her foot to stop the bleeding. I begin washing her foot with the Perrier, the water fizzing across her sole and thumb but flowing on top of the blood. I keep washing, absorbing all this marvelous topography of leg and knee. Her legs are long, autonomous objects. They're blessings. I can't help but notice that she is wearing Nevermore underpants — Dad's Poes end up close to everything! The bottle is empty, and Clare unstraps the cloth belt from her Far from the Madding Crowd. "I'll use this as a bandage."

"No, your foot isn't clean yet," I protest and go back inside to look for rubbing alcohol. Iodine. Anything. But the joint has nothing. Shit! I buy a six-pack of Perrier and then I am back down at Clare's feet, fizzing her flesh again — holding her ankle and using the hem of her skirt to dry her foot.

"You and Jesus — what a team," she says.

"I'll always remember what that guy taught me about foot care." I laugh, then add, apropos of nothing, "Just as I'll always remember the magic baby . . ."

Clare grabs my wrist. "You've seen Soda?"

I'm not really aware of what I just said, but my mind jumps: Perrier. Seltzer. Club soda. Then I realize Clare means the Lindy baby, Soda. The nanny catches my confusion — "Wait a minute! Everything you've told me so far is a lie, right?"

"Not lying," I say. "Acting."

Clare immediately gets that I was once an actor — a real one — and asks: "Were you any good?"

I pause, then nod. "I once had my own TV show."

She squints. "You don't look that old."

"I was just a kid, then the juice died," I say. "I had to do theater until Tokyo took over the theater district and Kabuki became the rage." I hold out my hand. "Can you stand? I'll help."

She shakes her head. "I'm fine. Tell me about your show."

I smile. *Every woman loves hearing about the electric days.* So I tell her. Because I have a larger narration in mind for you, all you need to know is that I once starred in a syndicated comedy called *The Man Who Respected Women* — costarred actually: I was the man-who-respected-women's kid brother. I didn't respect anyone, let alone females — but I stole the show. The few viewers we pulled in loved me. Everyone figured I'd grow into something. But the show died long before Hoover Dam. The network slotted us against Angela Lansbury and we got creamed during sweeps week.

"After the Blackout, why didn't you do Kabuki?" Clare asks.

I shrug. "I could never get the hang of those Nip moves. No. I've just spent the years drifting. I stage-managed on Off-Broadway. Then I ran a go-go girl bar. Then I put my acting skills to use and became a detective for a while. Then I raised an aviary of carrier pigeons. Then I hooked up with an ornithologist who wanted to breed a better bird."

I stop talking — I'm sick of the word *then*.

"What happened?" Clare asks.

"I got sick of feathers. Now I'm trying to make a living having visions."

"Any money in it?"

"Not yet. Only Rockefeller made any dough doing this, but I'm still hoping."

I pause, then tell Clare what happened to me one day last

spring — when I went into a trance and suddenly became a boy again, traveling above the country in an airplane. A jet. A DC-10. You'll never know what it was like when men and women and children flew together inside Air West and TWA. We seldom had the sense that we were flying — we were all so separate and nonchalant about being a mile high. We'd even pull down the windowshade and watch movies. Modern movies that were not only in color, but when you stuck the pair of rubber listening-tubes in your ears, you heard them as well. I remembered being on a night flight. I was about twelve years old and my network show had just been canceled. For some reason, I pulled the shade shut. Then I looked up to see they were screening the first film I had ever made. The title is too absurd to mention, but I will — *The Son from Mars.* That's the one I made when I was five. The thing was running when the stewardess came by with the drink cart. I was paging through a *Vanity Fair,* pretending to read.

"This is a pretty good movie," she whispered. "You should watch it."

This boy gave a sad smile to the woman. Then I realized that she didn't recognize me.

"There I was, entering puberty already a has-been," I tell Clare. "I was flying to a gig — but it wasn't a movie or TV show. It was a corporate imitation job. I had been reduced to that already. I had already played the son of a GM president for a *Detroit Free Press* spread, and even auditioned to be one of George Bush's grandsons, but the Republicans passed. I was hoping my network show would put an end to these slumming gigs, but I was fulfilling a long-standing commitment to play a Los Angeles executive's son — a man whose offspring I had played a few years before in New York. He needed me again in L.A. and I'd aged perfectly for the part."

"And the magic baby was aboard your airplane?" Clare asks.

I shake my head. "The baby happened several days later." I start washing Clare's toes, making no pretense of doctoring her wound. I just need something to do with my hands. This memory jacks me up. There I was — in my fake father's house in Echo Park getting briefed for the part — when an unexpected visitor showed up and they had to hide me. They left me in a room with a crib. I walked over and saw the baby.

The baby.

"I was eye level with this giant baby-head that was giving me the most incredible gaze," I tell Clare. "Even as a kid I recognized the cold wisdom in that stare. There was something so profound about that baby that I had to forget it immediately."

I pause. Take a deep breath. I just lied. I forgot nothing. I know what was profound about that baby. I'm about to admit this to Clare, but she grabs my arm: "I know a baby with a gaze like that." She blurts non sequiturs about the Lindy baby so rapidly that I can't focus on anything she is saying. Then in a moment that is both profound and comical — I am kneeling at Clare's feet, my fingers rubbing the soft flesh of her sole, feeling the bones, washing her foot cleaner than any woman's foot has ever been before — there in the night, a horse gallops up Fifth Avenue and stops half a block away under a gaslight. The animal has no saddle, so it's probably a runaway from a Chelsea stable. We watch the horse for a long time without speaking. And then, instead of telling Clare my secret, I take her hand and we both spontaneously start singing that old song Dylan wrote for Marianne Faithfull on *Dwarf Music:* "Wild, wild horses . . . couldn't drag me away."

Somehow this makes sense.

We sing "Wild Horses" as if there were some impending un-

knowable thing going on out there in the night — going on beyond the peripheries of our understanding, our sight. And this
sheer animal mystery has now at last stomped out of the shadows
to present itself to us. And what could be more mysterious than
whatever electricity is happening between Clare and me? People
aren't supposed to fall head-over-heels anymore, but perhaps love
is a Quantum Aberration of the Quantum Aberration that robbed
us of wattage to begin with.

"You're hurting me," Clare is saying.

I realize I'm crouched on the street rubbing her foot like it's
Aladdin's lamp. I stop. I'm about to speak. But I say nothing.
Then: "Stay here — I'll go find your shoes."

I walk toward her shoes, toward the horse. I can smell him.
He is panting by the curb, considering one of Clare's shoes as it
glimmers in the gaslight. The animal's ribs move in and out. He
watches me bend and pick up the shoe. His breath is hot. He
watches me walk across the street and search until I find the other
one. As I turn back, the horse dismisses me and trots away down
Seventeenth Street. I'm not reading mysticism into a simple mammal gaze. The horse really did just dismiss me.

Well, fuck that pony. That horse was just a horse, not a metaphor for love.

I take the shoes to Clare. She sits on the curb, wrapping her foot.
"Do you think the Lindys are spawning some secret race of

babies?" I ask. "And their children hold the long-lost electrons in their bodies like seeds?"

She smiles and answers my question with a question. "So you buy Con Ed's story that electrons are flowing backward in time?"

"I've delivered messages to Indian Point, and the power station is still running."

"Sending the current into the past?"

I shrug. I'm stalling.

"You're not one of those Tower Records freaks who believe all our current is flowing back through time to when Bob Dylan went electric at Newport?" she says.

"That would be ironic." This Dylan smiles.

"Cynicism is stronger than irony." Clare snorts. "The juice is flowing all right — they're just pumping the current up the Hudson to the Rockefeller estate in Pocantico."

"Right. And Winthrop, Jr., is watching reruns of *Miami Vice* on his VCR." I laugh. "All my life I've leaned toward Marx, but I do believe Con Ed."

She waves her hand. "Come on. I bet you're one of those guys who pick fights in bars over whether electrons are particles or waves."

I shake my head. "A woman is the only thing worth engaging in fisticuffs over." I raise my fists.

"Well, don't fight anyone over me." She laughs as she slips her uninjured foot into a flat. "So how did you end up nosing around the Lindy baby?"

I stall no longer and say, "I want to know if your Lindy is the man whose son I played in California." I say this all calmly. "It's been thirty-odd years."

I pause. Then I tell her the truth: "Look, when the electricity went, I realized something inside me was already gone. Something the baby took."

Clare looks confused. "What? What could a baby take from you?"

I don't answer right away. "A sense of success," I finally say. "Ever since that moment the cancer of failure has rotted me. I'm a has-been's has-been. For years I've walked around picturing Herman Melville in his post-Ishmael days. Talk about failure. I think in the end he worked as a postal inspector or something. . . ." I pause and frown. "Or was Walt Whitman the one who slung mail?"

Clare shrugs.

"Well, just imagine the weight of Melville's failure," I say. "The man beat his wife. The man even shot and killed his eldest son. Drove the younger son off to sail his dad's Pacific as a failed sailor and die a drunk cardsharp." I raise a finger. "Not that *Son from Mars* is equal to *Moby Dick*." I smile. "But Melville is my role model for failure. And when I replay being stared at by that baby, I become convinced it stole something from my psyche." I suddenly feel foolish. "Shit. I know this sounds like Post New Age bullshit."

Clare looks sad suddenly. "Oh, I know all about the Post New Age. My father wrote some books." She goes silent.

I'm about to tell her that I already know about her dad. Then I don't. I don't want this woman to feel violated by my sheldraking. Instead I find myself spitting: "I want to track down that Lindy child as an adult and get back what that fucker stole from me as a baby." I can't believe what I say next. "And if that fucker won't give it back — kill 'em."

Clare gives a dry laugh. "Fucker this. Fucker that. Kill, kill,

kill. Now you're talking like a nanny — want a toke of Vengeance, comrade?"

She lifts her other leg and puts her injured foot most of the way into her shoe. "Stop looking up my dress," she says.

"I admit nothing." I help her stand and she asks, "So you're sure Mr. Lindy of Jersey Bounce was the man in California?"

I nod my head vigorously, then ask, "Can you walk?"

Clare hobbles a few steps. "It looks worse than it feels." She begins limping downtown. "So what were you doing at Radio City last night? And why are you following me?" The nanny stops and presses both hands to her chest. "Do you think I was the Lindy baby and you have to kill me?"

"Oh no," I say. "You're a little too young."

"Why are you following me around?"

I lie. "I first saw you two days ago when you showed up on the porch of Big Pink."

She goes, "Big what?"

"On the Lindy's porch."

"And last night?"

"I live in the neighborhood."

"Yes. Sure," Clare says sarcastically. "Start over. Why do you think the Lindys could be the parents of the baby who stole your soul?"

"It's a long story, but the man whose son I played is a Lindy who's lived in both New York and Los Angeles. I checked some real estate records down on Chambers Street and think your Lindy is my Lindy."

She laughs, "*My* Lindy?"

I nod. "Was your Lindy ever in Los Angeles?"

"The baby is named after some mountains out there." Clare

goes silent for a moment, then abruptly turns. "Come on." She takes my arm and we begin walking/limping uptown.

"Where are we going?" I ask.

"Where I first met you," she instructs, dropping my arm. "Radio City."

"Why?"

"There are file cabinets up there. We can poke around and see if my Lindy is your Lindy."

"This is how Watergate started," I say.

"What do the Lindys have to do with that?"

"Not the Lindys," I answer. "Breaking and entering can lead to unnecessary complications."

"Maybe. But you're not Dick Nixon."

I think about that. "And you're not Gordon Liddy."

"Who's he?" she asks.

I laugh. "Thomas Edison's brother."

"Oh, please." She waves her hand. "Next you'll tell me he was Alexander Hamilton's lover. My mother warned me about electric-age guys like you jazzing poor girls like *moi* about plugs and currents and wattage."

5 modern bump and grind

NOT WANTING to jazz this innocent any longer, I flag down a carriage and we ride uptown, the horse clomping past a small parade of cleaning personnel trudging along the street with their plastic cans and mops. Clare and I hop out at Radio City. I feel great in my hopping. Like we're already lovers and New York is our metaphoric nocturnal oyster. Clare, however, is all business.

"Now here's what we're going to do," she says. "Go to the employee entrance. Just agree with whatever I say. When I give the signal, run for the stairwell."

But we find the double institutional doors chained shut.

"Damn!" Clare moans.

"We're not dead yet," I say. "Let's go to the main entrance."

"And do what? I don't want to use my ID."

"Don't worry, we'll use mine. I have a fake messenger ID from my gumshoe days."

We walk to the entrance proper, a dim lobby lit by a single lantern. Not that a chandelier would help — this lobby will always be dim. I remember coming here as a boy. I was being interviewed on some talk show, a program where viewers were content to watch nothing but talking heads. This lobby was dim when electricity burned and it's just as dim by candlelight. This dim-factor is because of an oppressive dark mural. I tell Clare how Raymond Hood allowed his lobby to be defined by it, a grim sepia mural that depicted the glory of the working man. Limited glory! There aren't any actors or nannies included in the tableau.

Vladimir Ilyich Lenin is missing too.

"Not that Lenin was an actor or nanny, of course," I say. "But underneath this long brown painting is Diego Rivera's original mural featuring Lenin."

"How do you know this stuff?" Clare asks as we approach the guard's station. "You don't look like a retro-Red."

I don't get a chance to answer — the Latino guard pacing up his volts on a treadmill answers for me: "Diego painted Lenin shaking hands with the peasants." He takes a deep breath, does more steps. "When Rockefeller saw it, he went apeshit and had it painted over."

"What did Diego say about that?" Clare asks.

I answer before the guard can. "Nothing. The Mexican got paid." The guard looks annoyed. I then flash him my fake messenger ID. "We have a message for one of the cleaners."

"Two of you?"

"It's a sing job."

He cranes his neck and squints at my ID again. He should just wave us in, but instead he asks, "Who?"

"Who who?"

"Who's the cleaner?"

Without hesitating, I say, "Dylan Washington."

"Ain't no Dylan Washington cleaning Radio City."

He's wrong. There is always a Dylan Washington working somewhere. I smile and say, "You know all the cleaners personally?" I figure he just wants to give me a hard time and then he'll let us go. But no! Slick Boy steps off the treadmill and escorts us up a wide stairway to a mezzanine. Then I get it: He's pissed that I didn't let him be the one to reveal the mural.

"Don't think you're the only cosmopolitan citizen around here," Clare whispers.

"What do you mean?"

"Lenin on the mural — big deal. I bet you don't know why Grant Wood of Iowa was so big on enchiladas suizas."

Huh? I shrug.

"Because he used to pal around with Diego Rivera," she says.

"So?"

"I've heard all about this mural. Lenin was the least of the travesties."

"What are you talking about?"

"At the top of the wall Rivera painted a scene of Mrs. Rockefeller and Mrs. Du Pont playing bridge while a herd of enlarged germs swarmed in their direction."

"Germs?"

"Yes — germs. They were — how do you say — anatomically correct. I mean they were scientifically exact illustrations of syphilis germs. That's what killed it for the Mex's mural."

Allissa never told me this. Clare has one-upped me on Radio City lore.

At the end of the mezzanine, we approach a group of cleaners hunkered around a lantern, eating sandwiches.

"Is this your idea of buying me dinner?" Clare whispers.

We're both hesitating at the edge of this gathering. Everyone here has dreadlocks — even a skinny Asian kid. No one looks up from their food. I was once an actor, but *dammit!* I hesitate like an amateur. I suppose I could just start singing "Happy Birthday" and just wing it when I get to the "Happy birthday, dear Dylan" part. But then, Clare suddenly struts forward — *what gives?* — and shouts, "Tah-dah!" Everyone pauses midbite, then continues chewing. Only after they swallow do they lower their bread. Silence. Then Clare starts to sing.

"Happy birthday to you . . ."

Her voice is clear and distinct when it doesn't crack. But surely our game will be up when she reaches, "Happy birthday, dear Dylan." But Clare switches languages and begins singing in what I assume is Japanese. Her melody becomes less and less recognizable as "Happy Birthday." The two women in the group go back to eating, but the men perk up. They watch Clare's hands as she caresses her chest. They watch her unbutton her blouse. Now the women abandon their aloof stance. They all lower their sandwiches as Clare slips off her top and begins belting out a song that bears absolutely no resemblance to "Happy Birthday." Not that the men care. Clare appears to be performing a full-fledged striptease. She puts a lot of English in her rotating hips, but this isn't really bump and grind. Her dance would be too weird for Las Vegas. Clare is not doing it postmodern either. There's something good-natured and loony about the way this nanny flings off her skirt. This nanny is stripping in defiance of Postmodernist Stripping. And Social Criticism Stripping. And Didactic Feminist Stripping. Clare is a woman apparently without a beef against American consumerism or the patriarchy.

I'm stating all this for the benefit of you young women. Young Ishmaels.

If I were addressing a bar full of compadres, I wouldn't talk about postmodernism, that's for sure. I'd say: "Boys, no digressions will keep me from giving you a description of Clare's lovely naked body. Consider her breasts. I'm seeing them with my eyes now, not just my brain. Let's consider together those large nipples — like the thumbs of babies. Look at the wine-colored areolas circling wide and fading nebulously across the skin of each breast proper."

Not that Clare's breasts necessarily have such nipples. I'm much too much the gentleman to assume that the specific circumference of her areolas are (or are not) of interest to you. Not that I'm not necessarily enjoying the act of witnessing them myself. I'm trying to think of what we'll do when she gets to the "Happy Birthday, dear Dylan" part of the song.

A song that has now changed into "Glow Worm." You know the tune, for sure. It's a song so old it is sung at the Metropolitan Opera. Dylan and the Band even covered it on the unreleased *Basement Tapes*. Clare herself suddenly realizes that this is the song that Mrs. Lindy is always warbling in a foreign tongue. And as Clare sings this song, I stop worrying about anything. Just smile as Clare sings this dear little prayer to our precious lost current: "*Glow little glow worm, fly of fire / like an in-can-des-cent wire / Glow for the female of the species / Turn on the AC and the DC . . .*"

Clare sings this delicious plea for electricity with her arms raised above her head, wildly swinging her rump, which — I have to tell you — is pleasantly large for her general body size. Clare has nurtured the kind of rump my father used to love to drape a George Eliot across.

I am certainly not obsessing on my father (or George Eliot for that matter) as Clare shimmies. For the first time in my life I am understanding the intense insectness of the song — *"Glow little glow worm, turn the key on / You are equipped with taillight neon . . ."* It is as if the base of this woman's spine can spin not only silk, but light as well — her body the thorax of a magical katydid.

And Clare does a final demented bump and offers the only part of her body still covered — her bandaged foot. As she unwraps the cloth, she wiggles her toes, and removes the bandage belting out, "Happy, happy birthday, dear Dylan."

There it is. "Dylan." Our gig is up . . .

". . . Happy birthday to you."

I see the male cleaners have all had dopey smiles on their faces — but suddenly they are all looking at the floor. A woman yells, "Dylan works on five." The other woman snickers. As if on cue, the men all begin viciously attacking their sandwiches.

Quick as can be, Clare drops down — grabs her Far from the Madding Crowd, saying, "Oh jeeze. Oh jeeze." She shoots me a glare as if I'm the one who whipped her shower curtain away while she was bathing. Is she acting? What did Clare think was going to happen when she finished? I don't get a single sheldrake about what's in her head. Later, Clare will tell me what happened. She'll tell me that as she removed the bandage — that final bit of linen — she was suddenly back with the barefoot babynapper in Jersey. She was replaying how she had bounced down those stone steps with the upper hemispheres of her brain pumped up on adrenaline — bracketed by cool, calm, murderous rage. She was really buzzing on Vengeance. She knew if she died at this moment, every part of her body would turn into coal, save her trigger finger — that bit of bone and skin would metamorphose into a curl of fire.

Clare turned down the stone curve and there was the barefoot girl —

Just standing there. The baby in her arms. Soda and the baby-napper were going eye-to-eye, the girl with her hand behind the baby's head in that ancient Dr. Spock position, a pose as classic as a Corinthian column.

Clare knew the barefoot girl was doing Cone Heart with Soda.

Clare was sure. Clare knew. Clare was sure and she knew, but she was suddenly bewildered too. Clare didn't believe she was jealous. Cone Heart is an exclusive experience, but one can't covet it exclusively. The angels circling God singing *Holy Holy Holy* are not jealous of each other in their joy. Jealousy is petty, and Clare's only petty thought was the smug delight of the vindicated — she now knew her own experiences with Cone Heart were real.

Cone Heart was real, not just a form of nanny burnout.

But did this shared Cone Heart with Soda make her and the barefoot girl equals? *Sisters?* Well, why not? Clare had literally worn this girl's shoes. Then the barefoot babynapper stuck out her lower lip and peered down at Soda and just groaned in pleasure. Clare had to turn away — this moment was too private. And as she looked away, the blood inside her ears started ringing and she felt her face flush. And then the drum started banging. *Vengeance. Vengeance. Vengeance.*

The nanny looked back, raising her gun. Aiming for the woman's head. The drum now banging, *Face off. Face off.* And the babynapper was standing there trembling, offering Soda to Clare.

Then the baby slowly rolled that gigantic baby head toward the nanny and gave Clare a remote glance — the child was denying her entrance to Cone Heart. Soda had merely glanced at the *surface* of Clare, as if the nanny were a painting. As if Clare were some mythical Grant Wood portrait, *Nanny with a Gat.*

The babynapper languidly leaned back against the railing with a dreamy look on her face, baby outstretched. Clare realized that she had penetrated through the heart of Vengeance and the only one left to shoot was herself.

Nope. She closed her eyes. Then slipped the borrowed Browning into the waist of her Far from the Madding Crowd, looking down at the woman's bare feet. They were small and white and vulnerable somehow. They reminded her of Mr. Lindy's feet. She took the baby.

Clare finds herself standing naked staring at her own feet. The nanny raises her injured foot and glances at the wound. She bets that Soda's barefoot kidnapper is still standing on that stairway in the dark, blissed out of her mind. Clare realizes that she has never gone as deep as that woman did into Cone Heart. Perhaps nannies — junkies — are so armored they are restricted to only catching glimpses, while other women can let Cone Heart enter them at ground zero. *What other women?* Just normal women. *But, who's normal?* Clare realizes that she's standing in front of an audience. *Are these women normal?* It hits her that she is naked — she's gotten naked in public just like her mother. Finally. *Mother must have felt Cone Heart for me. Cone Heart is what gave that woman the right and fortitude to stand naked for strangers. Mother should be standing here at Radio City. The barefoot girl too. Both women, naked hip to hip. But not me. Me being naked here is a travesty.*

Clare is crouched — still naked — as the guard says, "Hey, we got no problem here."

He's studying the freckles on her upper back, dazed out of his gourd. He bends down to pick up her Nevermore, for one moment looking as if he wants to stuff its thin black cloth into his mouth. "I'll take you guys up to Dylan's station," the guard says. He says this with enthusiasm. He's jolly even. Then he shines his lantern on his watch. "Shit." He motions us forward. "Come on." We follow — Clare crouched down, bundling her slip over her breasts while I hold up her skirt as cover. "Wait here," he says, stopping us. "I'll be back in a shake and take you up."

Clare stands and tries to focus her eyes. On anything. The guard just walks away, giving her an evil glance over his shoulder. The nanny takes my hand and hurries us to a door and then pulls me into a pitch-black stairwell. I hear her getting dressed in the dark.

"Need help?" I say.

"Stay where you are, buster."

"My intentions were honorable."

"Ha!" she shouts. Then I sense her body shuddering. I stay where I am. "I can't believe I did what I just did," she finally says. Then she whispers, "Mama. Mama. Mama. Oh, Mama." I touch her shoulder. Clare starts talking. She doesn't tell me about Cone Heart. She tells me about bump, about grind — "I remember when I was a kid in Japan and found out about how regular stripteases are done, I phoned my mother and asked why she didn't twirl her tassels like other strippers did when they got naked. 'That would be parody,' my mother told me. 'And parody hints at depth.' My mother then patiently explained that she objected to the occurrence of depth in performance because she felt it was a corruption of intent." Clare sighs. "Mom was just anti-Squat Theater. She was anti-Mabou Mines."

I start laughing.

"What's funny?" she asks. Her voice sounds bitter.

I tell Clare that it was my father who originated Lit Wear. After she does her *No / You're not serious / Oh wow*ing, I say, "So there was your mother embracing the Twentieth Century by stripping naked without depth, and there was my father embracing the Nineteenth Century by dressing kids in high lit."

"Think if it had been the reverse," Clare says.

"Like what?"

"Mom doing a meaningful strip and kids dressed in Postmod Wear."

Oh, Ishmaels! Perish the thought. Would you then all be named Foucault?

We feel our way up the dark stairs to Clare's office. I see the letters on the door: NBC. And laugh.

The Nanny Broker Company.

The god that turned off the world's electric lights has a sense of humor! As if asserting this, when Clare unlocks the door, we're flooded by instant light. Oh, it's only moonlight. But after the darkness of the stairwell, it hurts my eyes.

In one moment, Clare picks up a wastebasket and turns it upside down. "Empty."

"So what?"

"The cleaners have been here."

She begins jiggling the drawers of various desks. I notice the skirt of her Far from the Madding Crowd is on backwards and I tell her so.

"Big deal. Cancel my subscription to the *New York Review of Books.*"

"What are you looking for?" I ask.

"One that's locked." Jiggle. Jiggle. "Here. This will be the one." She jimmies the drawer open with a letter opener. There are small icons inside — tiny electric doodads like adding machines and cellular phones with pictures of Black Allah and the Virgin Mary rubberbanded around them. I also see kilo bricks of uncut Vengeance wrapped in tinfoil. Clare touches them with her fingertips. Gives a brief caress. Then she shoves the Vengeance aside and goes for the good stuff: The flashlights. The batteries. "There must be eight hundred dollars' worth of fertilizer here," I say.

Clare says nothing. Her mind is still flip-flopping between Vengeance. Batteries. Vengeance. Batteries. She plops two batteries into a flashlight — her hand suddenly shaking — and clicks on a beam of cold, beautiful light. She lets out a soft groan. *Light!* We all know that scientists claim this radiance isn't real AC/DC, but I remember those old Longlife White days and this flow of light looks electric enough for me. Clare keeps a small pool of it on the floor and heads to another room — walking the light the way other women walk their dogs.

· · ·

Dogs are on my mind as I hear a caninelike grunt. Guard dog? Then a soft singing sound — a cross between a song and a noisy farm animal. Clare takes a Glock from the gun rack and walks the flashlight to a storage closet. I follow. Inside, we find a tie-dye mummy. Seriously! It's a woman's shape wrapped in some sort of diaphanous purple, orange, and gold shroud. Clare bends down and lifts the fabric. *I've seen this nanny before — is she dead or just sleeping?* It's the walleyed nanny with the aboriginal forehead. Ms. Tattoos. Ms. Publish or Perish. This is the walleyed nanny I had sheldraked shooting up the corpse of the editor's wife in Washington Square Park. The nanny is dressed in some cheap flannel underthings, her Devil's Dictionary burnoose folded under her head. Her tattoos remind me of old-fashioned tire treads stained psychedelic.

"Dix?" Clare says, feeling her pulse.

I think Clare has just said *dicks*. "*Dicks* as in detectives?" I ask.

Clare looks up in disbelief. Then says, "Like Dixie Cup, dummy."

I shrug. "Is she dead?"

Clare shakes her head and stands. "It would take an old nanny-issue Colt to plug this gal." Clare uses her foot to cover the woman back up. "Dix is just overindulging herself with Vengeance."

"Has she OD'd?"

"Yes. No," Clare says with a shrug, then bends down and lifts Dix's eyelid. "She'll just be out of it until sunrise." She runs her finger along the out-of-it nanny's tattoos. "She's always on the needle," Clare says without emotion. "Dix had this done to hide her tracks."

That nanny shoots Vengeance in her forehead? I don't want to know.

We now enter Keegan's office. Two adjoining walls are lined with shelves.

"Are those cocktail shakers?" I ask.

Clare nods.

Behind the shakers are Keegan's totems — but not to electricity. The shelves hold no blow dryers wrapped in flowers. No incense in an electric toothbrush. There are just books. The same book. Not the same edition, but a hundred years' worth of reprintings. You could imagine Keegan paying homage to a baby book — say, editions of Spock. But see the rows of small red covers. Some bright. Some rusty. Some faded to the color of a good sunburn. Keegan's equivalent of Chairman Mao's Little Red Book. Keegan has a hundred-year collection of *Mr. Boston's Official Bartender's Guide.*

"The boss even owns the 'repeal of Prohibition' edition," Clare tells me.

I really know very little about this book — I worship the vine, not the cocktail. Clare informs me that *Mr. Boston's* was once Keegan's second American bible, after *Science and Health.*

"God bless Leo Cotton," Clare says.

"Who?"

"The editor for forty-nine editions. I think he was a Christian Scientist too. He edited *Mr. Boston's* in an old office across the street from the mother church. Keegan told me that a deaf woman may have only needed to read fifty pages of Mary Baker Eddy's

Boston Bible to have her ears healed, but a future bartender had to read all two hundred and fifty-nine pages of *Mr. Boston's* to really comprehend the alchemy of drink."

The nanny shines the beam across a bank of file cabinets. "File room."

"We search them?"

She nods.

"Where should I start?"

She slides open a file drawer and just stares into it.

"What's wrong?" I ask.

"I'm thinking," she says. "You go ahead and start searching."

I'm not sure what I'm looking for, but I start paging through the files of spreadsheets and financial statements. I get into my searching when I discover xeroxes from the electric days, xeroxes of checks, payable to NBC. Clare watches me pick up stacks and fan them open. It takes a while, but I find checks signed by Lindy.

Lindy Lindy Lindy.

Lindy vouchers from last year. Lindy twenty years ago. Lindy forever. The Lindys have been paying Nanny Broker Company for forty years, checks drawn from banks in Manhattan. Los Angeles. Jersey.

"What does this mean?" I ask.

Clare just looks blank. "I be no Sherlock."

"How many different nannies could the Lindys have had?"

Clare bites her lip. "It's company policy to rotate girls out of a family every six months."

"That means the Lindys may have had eighty different nannies."

"Sure," Clare says. She suddenly looks very happy. She is breathtaking in that state. "Why does this please me?" she asks.

"It means you aren't crazy — something is up with these Lindys!"

"Maybe," she says. "What about the other babies? Have the Lindys been having babies for forty years?" Then she looks panicked. "Cone Heart," she says. "Forty years' worth of Cone Heart?" She's talking to herself. "Have other nannies felt Cone Heart?" She looks up. "You don't know what I'm talking about, do you?"

I just shrug as we walk back into Keegan's office. I know lots about Cone Heart, of course, but I don't want to let on. Then I'd have to confess my sheldraking. *Jesus, already I'm lying to my love.*

"I desperately need a hit of Vengeance," she says.

"Clare, just thank God humans feel the need to keep records." I wave the papers. "If we were both wearing Bartlebys we could do a jig in honor of bureaucrats and paperwork."

She stops and leans against Keegan's door. "To hell with pharmaceuticals. I want you to dance without your Bartlebys." Clare says this with a smile as she shines the light my way — puts me in the spot.

I'm surprised at first. Then: How arousing electric light is! You won't catch me saying, *"I would prefer not to. . . ."*

I have to tell you that I'm *turned on* by the flashlight. I've never been able to imagine light as a wave. I believe on the photon level it surely is nothing but jagged lines and searing heat. On the other hand, this Dylan does not observe life on the photon level. I live on the level of flesh, and bathed in this light I say proudly: "The flesh is weak."

"You saw me dance," Clare says. "Your turn. . . ."

I suddenly don't know what to do. "What about. . . ?"

"Dix?" Clare says. "She'll be Vengeancing until the roosters crow."

Roosters. Crowing. I try to just go with this idea. I begin unbuttoning my shirt. But I need a rhythm.

Masculine music.

I hear one of those stomping Russian folk dances. I begin stamping my feet. Like a Cossack. I begin singing out, "*Sergei. Sergei. Nyet. Nyet.*" (The only Russian words that come to me.) I confess to you that I don't feel exuberant. What I saw of Clare's dance was glorious in its unselfconscious fervor. I feel like the Joseph Stalin of self-consciousness. But I will not report my self-consciousness. Instead, should I tell you about my body? Is it fine? Old? (I do puff Twenty Something, remember.) In good shape? An embarrassment? It matters to many, but surely not to you. For you, alone, I will kick off my shoes. Twirl my undershirt. Unbelt my trousers. And tell you the most honest thing I can —

I don't want to undress with an erection.

I have no particular shortcoming, but it seems comical. Like Pinocchio. I'd say fifty percent of men feel this way. I am hoping it will lower as I take off my Levi's (note: today no Lit Wear), but the damn thing doesn't. Bathed in electric light, it is a lighthouse. And while displaying the pinnacle of my mannish light, what more appreciative gesture can I make but salute Alexander Graham Bell. You know Bell invented the dial tone, the receiver, the wrong number. But did you know he also invented a telephone that sent messages with light? Yes. The telephone was a by-product of Bell's search for the perfect valentine for his wife. She was deaf, you see. Mrs. Alexander Bell was deaf from birth. Bell spent his life searching for a way to talk with her. He worked with light, believing he could somehow send her his voice through her eyes.

"Now just a minute, Dylan," one of you says. "Just whose

story are you telling, anyway — yours? Clare's? Or Alexander Graham Bell's?"

Well, your story in a way, dear girl. Against all odds of our age, I've fallen in love. Why should this state stop with me? Why not you too? Why shouldn't a man love your essence enough to build you a telephone of light?

Or at least sing to you as I am singing to Clare, switching from *nyet-nyet* to an old song from a specific time. A cartoon song from a cartoon time. A song from the Reagan days, when I was born. Talk about deep cartoon! I sing this song in honor of Clare and in honor of myself. My soul hadn't yet been snatched by some modern baby. And my song has nothing to do with Bob Dylan. I don't know the name of the group that recorded it, except I remember that the two women singers wore beehive hairdos — a retro gesture, because beehives hadn't been in fashion since the Clairol sixties. And their song was called "Planet Clare." And I'm singing it to the Clare who circles me with a flashlight: "*She came from Planet Clare / She came from Planet Clare.*"

My Clare sets her flashlight down and starts clapping. Then Keegan's office door opens.

A woman walks in.

And she's holding a gun.

6 animal magnetism

SUDDEN GLIMPSE of a woman-shape. In a dress. Devil red.

"Dix!" Clare shouts.

But no. An older woman — no tattoos — Kathleen Keegan gripping a Colt Diamondback, hip level.

"Ms. Keegan!" Clare shouts. "It's us."

The woman arches an eyebrow. "Us?" She keeps her pistol horizontal.

I give a quick sheldrake, but her skull broadcasts chaos. She is tripping. But how can that be? Kathleen Keegan was once a classy dame, not a doper. I was just a boy when I knew her, but I *got* her eminence.

Not that Keegan recognizes me. She doesn't give this naked Dylan a second glance — her eyes doing a dot-dot-dot to the stack of old Lindy vouchers on the desk, each one signed by either Gordon or Thalia Lindy.

"Now you know," she announces.

Know what?

"Know what?" Clare asks.

Wait! Let's ask one hundred questions, but enough of standing naked. I start for my trousers at the same time that Clare walks toward the gunwoman with her arm extended, saying, "Give me the piece, Ms. Keegan."

But the older woman jerks — her dress a red flare. Bullfighter's cape. *Olé!* Gunshots. I feel each one in my teeth. Clare and I both drop and roll into balls on the floor as Keegan shoots up the bookshelves. Bullets thudding in the spines of *Mr. Boston's*.

She stops. I hear a rapid click, click, click, Keegan whispering, "Flaming-shit-in-hell."

Clare and I both look up. Like a Mafia gunslinger, Keegan is already reloaded, spent casings at her feet along with a dozen pink squares. What's that, dice? Sugar cubes? As Keegan picks them up, I stand and again continue toward my pants. I am a stubborn naked man.

"Freeze!" Keegan flicks the cylinder shut Matt Dillon–style, grunting, "I'll shoot."

"Do what she says!" Clare yells. "Forget your slacks. They're not bulletproof."

"Yes. You'll not be needing trousers for our conversing," Keegan says. Then looks puzzled. "Whatever got into you? You're in the temporal world now. Surely you realize that?" Keegan sticks a sugar cube in her mouth. "The Lord loaned you that temporal body, but never forget what happened to Christ's same-such vessel."

Huh? "My 'vessel' has always been in the temporal world," I say with irritation.

Keegan just sucks on the cube.

I have to tell you, Ishmaels, in my life as a man-about-town (or "vessel-about-town"), I've been mugged three times by pistol.

Allissa Sontag once even poked a 9mm Smith & Wesson at me in a room at the Chelsea Hotel. Each gunpoint encounter was freaky, but I never really believed that I was going to be shot. Each pistol was only a theoretical gun. A gun of the mind. But now I'm naked. Nothing on my mind now except Keegan's very real, more-than-conceptional Colt Diamondback.

The red gunwoman herself now peers at Clare, saying, "After forty years it's going to end tonight. And I won't let you ruin it."

"Ruin what?" Clare asks — irritated, crossing her arms.

"I love you like a daughter," Keegan says (Clare rolls her eyes). "But I will still cut you down." Then she snorts. "That's a good one — 'I love you like a daughter.' Can you imagine me, the originator of *alienated child rearing,* raising a kid of my own?"

Clare has no answer. But she peers into Keegan's eyes. "Your pupils are big as saucers. What are you on?" She turns to me and says, "Vengeance doesn't do that."

"Don't tell me what sweet-Joseph-and-Mary vengeance is or isn't," the gunwoman snarls as she sucks another sugar cube, adding, "You dog-faced loser."

Keegan says those hateful words to Clare — to my Clare — drawing out each syllable with violence. But the nanny stays poker-faced, saying, "I wasn't talking to you. I was talking to Dylan."

Keegan looks at me and spits, "Dylan? How common!" She swats her hand. "I suppose you're convinced you're really named after Dylan Thomas instead of you-know-who." Without waiting for an answer, the red *pistolero* raises her free arm and wipes her forehead, saying, "I may love you like a daughter, Clare, but chuck it. I love the man like a husband."

"Who?" Clare asks without emotion. "Who do you love?"

Keegan turns to me again as if I'm supposed to answer. For

the first time I get a good look at her eyes. Jesus! Her pupils are gigantic. Mickey Mouse eyes. She's ripped!

When I don't answer, the gunwoman says, "Gordon. Gordon Lindy, of course," pronouncing his name in a steely voice. "You will not deny us the happiness we can finally have, Clare. I won't allow it — for his sake." Keegan then flips her gun at my business. "Mrs. Eddy sent you as a witness, then, Dylan?"

I shrug. What's my penis got to do with anything?

"It's about time Mrs. Eddy sent an angel to witness what I've been through," Keegan says to Clare.

Wait. *Mrs. Eddy* is Mary Baker Eddy — Mrs. Christian Science herself. Christ, can Keegan really be hallucinating that I'm a naked angel? My neighbor Curry Nolan smokes a drug that makes women think he's an angel, but I've never taken a toke.

"I'll be a witness," a low voice rasps.

I jerk. *Whozzat?*

"I'll witness everything," says the new voice. The voice of the tattooed nanny. She staggers into the room minus her shroud, with a Glock raised in her fist.

"Dix!" Clare shouts. "Watch out, the boss is packing."

Dix slides across the room, wearing her crummy flannels, leading with her head, as if her forehead with its blue-green aboriginal zigzags and doo-dah is what propels her forward. Then she stumbles. Catches her balance. Continues weaving across the room, chanting, "Vengeance! Vengeance! Vengeance!" Then she flops down behind the desk and goes quiet.

Keegan sighs. "So Dix is in on it too?"

Dix bangs her Glock down on the desktop.

"In on what?" Clare asks. "Dix is just zonked on Vengeance."

The tattooed nanny suddenly starts laughing, slapping the surface of the desk, making the gun bounce around. It's disconcerting to see the woman's walleyes simultaneously looking at Clare with her left and Keegan with her right. "Swell party!" Dix giggles, picking up the Glock. "When do we get laid?"

"Put the gun down," Keegan orders. Whatever drug this gal is on, it doesn't promote comradeship with those zoned on Vengeance. Keegan looks as cheerful as Queen Victoria.

But Dix just swats her free hand "Sure, boss. The gun goes down." She clunks the Glock to the desk, but continues to fondle the grip.

"I forgot that you nannied the Lindys nearly twelve years ago, Dix," Keegan says, then squints at Clare. "How did the two of you discover the child's secret?"

"What secret?" Clare asks. "That the Lindys needed a nanny forty years ago?"

"Chuck the innocent act, Clare," Keegan growls, waving her Colt at the young nanny.

Clare doesn't respond, but Dix slaps the desk. "What secret?"

Keegan gives a sad smile. "My words take twice as long to reach you as they do Clare?"

Dix ignores the question and begins ranting, "Secret? Secret? You think we're secret babynappers? You think we'd give up Vengeance to go nap some little shit-bundle?" Dix raises the Glock. "I ain't no babynapper." Then she stands up — her navel sticking out between her waistband and undershirt — and sings, "*Shoot 'em if they're Daisy / Shoot 'em if they're Shelly / Shoot 'em in the brainpan / Shoot 'em in the belly. . . .*"

Then she stops. Starts coughing. Collapses on the chair.

"You're a kip, Dix," Keegan says. "You and Clare both put on a good pony show, but can it now." She points the Colt at Clare. "After forty years the drama is about to end and he'll be free, and I refuse to let you two louse things up."

I see a vein jumping very clearly in the meat of Keegan's outstretched palm. Dark déjà vu! I remember a vein jumping like that just before Allissa Sontag pulled the trigger. *My God, I won't let this woman shoot my beloved.* My only play to is be an angel. If this old hophead wants a heavenly messenger, she'll sure as hell get one. I told you I was once an actor. I turn on the adrenaline and ham it up good. I'm an electric-age guy, but I don't bark something tough-guy and famous like Humphrey Bogart or John Wayne. This naked angel has the Gideons Bible on the brain. I intone a call: "KEEGAN!"

I'm aware that name is not found in the Bible, but I just feel the word's power in my voice. *Keegan. Keegan. Keegan.* It's a percussive word, making a naked guy feel Old Testament supreme. Goddamn, if Keegan wants an angel, an angel she'll get. And my voice cuts deeper than narcotics. Even Clare freezes up, feeling the power in my call. Dix collapses back into the chair. And Keegan lowers the Diamondback slightly.

My call means *Stop.*

My call means *Don't get an angel of heaven pissed at you.*

Jesus, I feel so much heavenly power that I'm suddenly standing here with a hard-on.

The gunwoman moves first. She turns to Clare. "Just as I suspected, he's total AM."

Huh?

Clare gives a cold laugh. "Dylan's penis is a radio?"

Dix suddenly slaps the desk. "Damn right — and broadcasting top ten!"

Ha! Who needs electricity? I agree!

Keegan flips her gun at my business again. "Explain AM to the girls, Angel Dylan."

I just mutter, "WNEW." *Or was that an FM station?*

"AM is Christian Science shorthand for Animal Magnetism," Dix warbles from the desk.

Keegan looks over with her saucer eyes and nods.

I can't believe it, Ishmaels. It's crazy enough that I am standing here naked with a hard-on held at gunpoint by a stoned Christian Scientist. But we're all going to discuss *animals with magnets?*

"God revealed Animal Magnetism to Mary Baker Eddy in 1863," Dix says.

Keegan looks impressed. "You know the date?"

Dix shrugs. "I took a Learning Annex course on Mary Baker Eddy."

"Whyever would you do that?" Keegan asks.

Dix gives a halfhearted shrug. "To impress you if it ever came down that I'd have to do something chickenshit like impressing the boss." Then Dix drops her head to her desk and starts hyperventilating, making little *whoop whoop whoop* sounds.

"Sweet mother, you nannies do frap on your Vengeance," Keegan remarks, sucking on a pink cube.

"You may be a Christian Scientist, but you're not a crazy one," Clare says. "What's in the sugar?"

"The essence of the Science," Keegan says, widening her eyes, like someone suffering from Graves' disease. "Freebased Animal Magnetism. You should know about AM, Clare. Everyone has it in its nonnarcotic form. It's generated in the middle of the brain. My brain. Your brain. Every New Yorker's brain."

Keegan sticks the gun casually under her arm. "Mary Baker Eddy taught us that Animal Magnetism is the hormonal force that draws all human thinking away from Spirit."

She pulls the gun out again. "It's the pull of Fame, Financial Security, Adventure, Health." She pauses. Says, "Sexual Satisfaction," giving a wink to my dick. "And, of course, Sedition, Heresies, Rebellion, and Wrath." She waves her free hand. "Explain that these conditions are not necessarily Evil, but that the idolatry of them always is."

I look at Clare. "The idolatry of them always is." What I really want to say: *Great. I got sheldraking. Clare has Cone Heart. And you have Animal Magnetism.*

"Hold it, partner," Dix interrupts. "Captain Jesus didn't talk of Animal Magnetism. That term ain't in the real Bible."

Keegan raises her eyebrows over dilated Mickey Mouse eyes. "What's the real Bible?"

Dix smiles. "The one you find in motels." She pounds the desk again, bumping the gun. "I know about the Good Book. And it sure ain't the Good News. I have a pale rider tattooed on my back to prove it." (That rider again! Does that particular tattoo have something to do with my black Muybridge stallion?) "That grim jockey starts on my shoulders," Dix says, reaching with her free hand over her collar, "and rides down to the left cheek of my ass."

"Which I'm sure you'd like me to kiss," Keegan remarks. "I have to insist to you all that Animal Magnetism is a real phenomenon. For more than a hundred years Christian Scientists have been taught to avoid Animal Magnetism, but the chemist I hired to manufacture Vengeance was a Christian Scientist who shared her secret with me. Animal Magnetism is a fundament that can be distilled. After only one hit, you're graced with the epiphany that the only way to transcend Animal Magnetism is to thoroughly embrace it and thus pass through it." She pauses to let that sink in. "I'm discreet. I keep my intake to myself. But I've taken a hit of AM every day for the past twenty years. This is why I've always seen my nannies for what they are."

"Oh, please, Ms. Keegan," Clare says with disgust. "We're simple homicidal child care workers — you need drugs to see that? Why are you on it now? I'm a simple nanny. And Dix is too."

"I'm on it because I only have a conscience when I'm straight." Keegan laughs. Then adds with mock-dramatic seriousness, "I mean I am not a monster" — emphasizing *monster* with a combination brogue and a quiver that reminds me of recordings of Eleanor Roosevelt. "If I only see you as pure Animal Magnetism, I can shoot you both without guilt after I tell you the story."

The young nanny rolls her eyes. "Fine. Okay. So what does my Animal Magnetism look like?"

Keegan considers a comment and says, "You're straight Sedition and Wrath."

Clare gives a snort. "No hints of Sexual Satisfaction?"

Keegan peers at Clare seriously, saying, "A little . . . ," while wiggling her free hand.

"So why tell us a story before you pop us?"

"So you understand why you must die," Keegan says. "This is a technique I learned from experience. You remember how I told you that I shot my father's dog?"

Clare nods.

"Before I pulled the trigger, I sat on a fence and told the beast why I was going to do what I was going to do. I spoke for most of the evening. Then I found I could shoot him."

"Ha!" Dix laughs. "Why don't you just smoke a can of Kennel Ration and realize our true Canine Nature?"

Keegan points her Diamondback at Dix — Clare starts waving her hands to distract her, sighing. "So what's the story you need to tell us?"

Keegan pauses, then says almost triumphantly: "How the Lindy child has both physically and mentally remained a six-month-old baby for forty years."

Neither Clare nor I reacts — that's as crazy as Christian Science hallucinogens.

"You have trouble comprehending that?" the gunwoman asks. "The baby was six months old in 1982. And the baby stayed six months old in 1983. And stayed six months old in 1984. And in 1985. Need I go on? The baby has been a six-month-old baby for forty years."

Silence.

Dix breaks it. "Big fuckin' fancy that," she says playfully, then starts sucking the air to produce rude snorts.

Keegan ignores the disturbance. "I'll say it again: The Lindy baby has stayed a baby for forty years."

But now Clare is the one laughing. "Great. A drunk walks into a bar and says to the bartender, 'Heard the one about the middle-aged baby?'"

Keegan swings her Diamondback in front of the light. "I never joke," she says.

The gun's shadow is now as big as a billboard.

"Or to be precise," she adds, "I never joke about the baby."

Clare just twirls her hair, affecting boredom. "So if Soda is forty years old, why can't the rug rat talk and walk?"

Keegan frowns. "To answer your question for the hundredth time — the Lindy baby is both physically and mentally six months old. The Lindy baby has radiated *complete* Baby AM since the years when Ronald Reagan was America's president."

Dix suddenly screams, "Leave the Gipper out of it!"

Huh? What does she care about Ronald Reagan?

The tattooed nanny pops up, her gun raised. Immediate gunshot — Keegan's shooting. You never get used to this noise. It jerks your neck. Your belly. *A hard-on sure stays down.* As I'm reacting, I see Dix jerk her fist up and down in a brief spastic frug. Her Glock flies to the floor. I note a little play of smoke puff across the room. A miniature cirrus cloud. Then I smell a smell that nostalgically reminds me of laundry left too long in an electric dryer.

Then I envision a flower.

Not for any sweet smell. But as a visual. There's a new swirl and color below Dix's forehead tattoos. A hideous chrysanthemum in the middle of her face where her nose once was. Dix's eyes have been jerked from their separate east-west orbits to looking dead-on.

"You next, Clare?" Keegan shouts. "Stay!"

Clare stays. I see her swallowing. She's gobbled some Vengeance.

The red gunwoman walks over to the desk. "Day and night, Dix, your AM was straight Fame, Sexual Satisfaction, and Sedition. Fame. Sexual Satisfaction. Sedition." Keegan places her hand on the crown of the dead nanny's head, saying, "You always did give me the creeps." Then she pushes the dead woman facedown on the desk. "Why are you nannies so goddamn ugly?" Keegan asks with a shudder.

Oh my love! That Clare has to take such shit from this red-dressed fossil.

But I see Clare standing there rigid, with narrow eyes, chewing the inside of her cheeks. She looks completely heartless. Keegan has a similar fever of malice going, but there's some spite around her edges. And spite is weakness. If Clare had a gun right now, Keegan would get plugged. No contest.

Clare finally speaks. She says, "So tell me about the little shit-rag before you shoot me." She says coolly, "Tell me about the oldest baby in the world."

7 tales from the reagan era

ISHMAELS, PICTURE me on a stage. Not a big one — not Radio City Music Hall with kicking Rockettes. A smaller one. Off-Broadway. Really really Off-Off-Broadway. Might as well make it the old SoHo Performing Garage. Picture this NBC office as the set. And your Dylan stands center stage playing a naked man mistaken for a naked angel.

The woman who is doing the mistaking is holding the angel at gunpoint. Kathleen Keegan is packing a Colt Diamondback revolver. She stands stage right wearing a fireplug-red dress. The gunwoman is hallucinating on some Christian Scientist narcotic. But she's not the only druggie up here. Clare, standing stage left, is high on Vengeance.

If you draw a line from Keegan to me to Clare, you get an equilateral triangle. If you draw a line from Keegan to me to Clare to the dead nanny lying facedown on that desk plunked at the rear of the stage, you get a parallelogram.

There is maybe twelve feet between Clare and me, but it seems like psychic miles. See her head cocked 65 degrees from the audience, transfixed on Dix's body.

Hear Keegan fire off the first line: "You'll think I'm stone mad when I tell you the Lindy baby was born with teeth."

Teeth? *A baby was born with teeth?* Yes, we're Off-Broadway for sure . . .

Clare looks irritated at the theatrics. "So a forty-year-old baby was born with dentistry." She sighs. "And what else? Little bat wings? Six legs?"

"You're missing the point, and you'll die for it," Keegan remarks. "I'll tell you again that the Lindy baby was born with a complete set of teeth."

Clare weighs Keegan's words, remembering Mrs. Lindy's pouch of teeth. "Teeth made Soda eternally six months old?" she asks, her voice edgy. Could be sarcasm. Could be rage at being held at gunpoint.

"No," Keegan answers, switching gunhands. "Teeth had nothing to do with it. After a year the Lindys had a dentist pull all the teeth, but the baby stayed a baby."

Clare crosses her arms, now staring at Dix. "So when was Soda born — 1982?"

"The Lindys' baby was born in December of '81," Keegan explains. "The baby aged until May of '82. Then stopped."

Keegan says this and we're all stationary. Then Clare walks toward the facedown dead nanny at the desk. Simultaneously, Keegan's gun arm darts up, but Clare kicks Dix's pistol across the floor, then reaches with her left hand to take Dix's left, raising the limp palm to her own belly and squeezing.

"So let's assume you're not just some hallucinating Christian Scientist," Clare says, facing Keegan. "Let's assume you're telling the truth. Let's assume you're telling history — you're telling us that Soda was born forty years back, when electricity still ran."

Keegan looks at Clare holding Dix's pale hand and considers this soft-boiled scene. Is the young nanny exhibiting nanny sisterhood? Sisters postdeath?

"The answer is *yes*," Keegan says after a moment. "I am telling you that the Lindy baby was born when electricity flourished."

"*The Lindy baby. The Lindy baby,*" Clare repeats, jerking Dix's hand with her pronouncements. "Is Soda the eternal baby, or do the Lindys have another rug rat stashed somewhere?"

Keegan shakes her head. "The Lindys have only had one baby, and that baby was born with the name Avadoot."

Clare drops Dix's hand. "Ava — *what?*"

"Avadoot," Keegan says again. And then spells it, accenting each letter with the barrel of her Colt. "Avadoot was the first baby I ever cared for. The Lindys were the family that my pregnant cousin came from Ireland to work for."

Clare nods, now using both arms to take up Dix's slack arm and hand. "So your Uncle pulled you from the bar — what was it called?"

"The Lost Weekend."

"Right. The Lost Weekend. You were pulled from the Lost Weekend to take her place and care for the Lindy's shit-bundle?"

Keegan nods. "Good-bye pulling pints. Hello diapers."

Clare frowns. "How could you accept Tooth Baby? All us working nannies know that you knew nothing about babies at first —"

"My initial lack of prenatal knowledge is legendary," Keegan admits.

"But surely even a barmaid knows six-month-old babies don't have teeth," Clare states.

The gunwoman shakes her head. "For a member of the Lit Wear generation, you're so unread! Mrs. Eddy's *Science and Health* contains dozens of accounts concerning teeth. Ninety-year-old women grow new sets of grinders all the time. To Gordon and Thalia Lindy, having a baby with teeth was just so . . ." She searches for words. "So trendy. So postmodern. Gordon and Thalia even tried to convince Cindy Sherman to snap some baby pictures."

Where is Keegan going with this?

"The Lindys didn't always live in New Jersey, you know," Keegan says. "They had a loft in SoHo."

Ah ha. That's why Keegan started doing art-speak. Hell, Angel Dylan may have been conceived up in Heaven, but he was born down below on Wooster and Grand in SoHo, in the days when that neighborhood of narrow streets and cast-iron Palladian buildings was in its Big Art/bigger bucks splendor.

"Were the Lindys artists?" Clare asks, gripping Dix's hand tighter.

"What you want to ask is: Did they see your mother doing her striptease art gallery act in the eighties?" Keegan says with a smile.

Clare doesn't respond.

"Maybe they saw her." Keegan shrugs. "Although the Lindys weren't artists themselves, they were yuppies." Keegan pronounces that antiquated word with a condescending tone. "They fancied themselves as a New Wave Fred Astaire and Ginger Rogers."

"Who're they?" Clare says.

Keegan just spits out the word, "Dancers." That's it.

"Just *dancers?*" I say. "Those two defined dance in the Twentieth Century."

Keegan shrugs. "Fred Astaire was never my idea of Johnny Handsome."

"Ginger Rogers was no hot dish either," I say. "But when those two danced — all beauty bets were off."

Clare clears her throat. "So Fred Astaire and Ginger Rogers are responsible for the Lindy's baby being freeze-dried at six months?"

"Get serious, Clare," Keegan barks.

The young nanny tugs Dix's flaccid arm with her left hand and rests her right on Dix's back. "Or did electricity freeze the baby?"

Keegan's eyes are buggy, but she still looks thoughtful. "No," she finally answers. "Electricity had nothing to do with it." Then she raises the Colt and gives a zonked-sounding laugh. "Or maybe I'm wrong. After all, it was in the Reagan era that all these new electric devices were invented — VCRs. PacMan. Touch banking. Color TVs."

Then Keegan starts talking faster — as if Animal Magnetism is a speedy drug. "Not that either Lindy understood the spirit of holy electronics. Gordon worked for Ozu Electronics, ugly stepbrother of Sony and Toshiba, and spent the Reagan years promoting the needleless turntable, while Thalia was a VP for the networks who wrote memos predicting that HBO was a passing fad." Keegan gives a snort. "Those two both backed the wrong horses." Then she waves her gun contemptuously at my angelic nakedness as if it were just horsey business, saying, "But those yuppies knew even less about raising a baby than they did about electricity."

Ishmaels, that Y-word again!

"Not that I was any more superior than they were," Keegan says. "I was, after all, a yuppie nanny. And before that, the Lost Weekend was a yuppie watering hole."

Yup. Yup. Yup. Hey, Ishmaels, I bet you think that term is as outdated as *Wobblies.* But in 1982, New Yorkers were still undecided whether this new leisure class was to be called *yuppies* or *yumpies.*

"But you know, truth be told," Keegan says, "mixing a perfect martini takes more skill than caring for a baby."

She pinches the stem of an invisible cocktail glass.

"Besides, Avadoot never cried or fussed," she continues. "I'd spend my afternoons transfixed by brushing Avadoot's little choppers." She chuckles. "A nanny didn't need a pistol in those days, just a toothbrush."

Clare's right hand is now resting on the desk, to the right of Dix's body. "So with all this dental hygienics, after six weeks didn't you or the Lindys realize the baby wasn't growing . . ."

"It took four months, if you can believe that," Keegan says. "Not that I or the Lindys were thick. They were just obsessed with their yuppiness — their faxes, their portfolios, their junk bonds — while I was obsessed with my nanniness. We all found rhythm and comfort with that baby's babyness."

Keegan's voice now sounds lucid. Enunciating clearly. Animal Magnetism must be a trampoline drug like nitrous oxide: up/down, up/down.

"After about four months," Keegan continues, "it started to give me the creeps how ugly and ungainly the other babies in the neighborhood had become. The mothers pushed them through the brick streets in their prams like chunks of rolling pork. But then it came to me that these other babies were growing, Soda was not."

She suddenly jerks the gun over her head as if she'll start shooting out the lights. "And everyone from Mary Baker Eddy to Penelope Leach assures us that babies are put on this earth to grow."

"Unless they're midgets," Clare states, moving Dix's hand for emphasis.

"But Avadoot's limbs were proportioned perfectly," Keegan says. "The child was no dwarf."

Then the old gunwoman looks at Clare. Gives a shudder. And pops another hit of Animal Magnetism. What — she's seeing Clare as Clare instead of as straight Sedition and Wrath?

"When I expressed my concern to Thalia and Gordon," Keegan resumes, "they only argued that Avadoot's metabolism was just slow." Keegan then points the Diamondback at Clare. "Your father came up with the phrase 'Inside Child,' didn't he?"

Clare nods, making Dix's hand wave.

"To bastardize your pop's terminology," Keegan purrs, "what would a woman's Inside Nanny say about the Lindy baby?"

Clare shrugs, Dix waves.

"My Inside Mrs. Eddy said that all of us get sick because doctors say we are sick," Keegan says rapidly. "All of us grow, age, and die because we see others aging and dying. But what could a Christian Scientist do? I couldn't very well have a practitioner come and tell the baby, 'Grow up. Grow up this instant.' No. I was forced to become Anti–Mrs. Eddy and do what no Christian Scientist had ever done before: telephone a doctor."

She gives me a look like *My last statement should have significance* — her pupils now remind me of chocolate mint cookies.

"So I lugged out the Bible of telephoning, the Yellow Pages." Turning to me, Keegan — Ms. Cartoon Eyes — says: "Tell Clare that this book had nothing to do with Asians, Angel Dylan."

This angel is about to speak, but first I realize I need a more steadfast image of an angel to battle the cerebral chaos of Keegan's bad trip. Outside Radio City are dozens of naked Art Deco angels, each one probably modeled after Nelson Rockefeller. That's how I'll stand. With Art Deco strength. Art Deco grace. "The Yellow of the pages referred to their color," I say in an elegant voice. I'm Rockefelleresque supreme.

"Yeah. Yeah. Yeah. I know how the pages in the phone book were the color of pee," Clare says.

So much for elegance.

"I once saw one in a shrine," she adds, wiggling Dix.

"Well, I opened the Yellow Pages to *Doctor*," Keegan says, opening an invisible book. "But no telephone numbers appeared — just the instructions to *see Chiropractors, Dentists, Optometrists, Physicians & Surgeons, and Veterinarians*. What did those designations mean?"

"The baby had teeth, I would have tried a dentist," Clare chirps merrily.

"Sarcasm will shove you closer to the timber," says Keegan.

Clare's right arm is now still — very still. "That was whimsy, not sarcasm."

Keegan gives a slow smile. "How would you like a little sarcastic bullet in your belly? My eyes see your pure Animal Magnetism — I'm dying to shoot."

"Well, then hurry up with your shitty little story," Clare says, and makes Dix's hand give a contemptuous wave.

Keegan shifts as if she's listening for something, then begins to bop her head. When she captures the cadence she is after, she continues. "So there I was trying to find the correct M.D., and I remembered that Biblical joke that ends with the punch line 'Physician, heal thyself.'"

Keegan gives a flipped-out laugh.

"A physician finally told me I wanted a pediatrician. So I made an emergency appointment with a man of that profession who had an office up in the Puck Building." She quickly pops another cube of AM and narrows her eyes at Clare. "The waiting room was full of screaming babies, but the minute I entered with Avadoot, they all stopped."

Then the gunwoman abruptly steps out of the light, and returns carrying an ice chest in her free hand.

"All this chin music," she mutters, "is making me hoarse." She sets the bucket on the extreme corner of the desk, far from Dix, and picks out an ice cube, then pops it in her mouth.

"Every baby shut up when we walked in," she continues. "Not a peep. The silence was that immediate. Total." She pauses. "But then the room was too quiet," Keegan whispers. "Too empty. I knew Avadoot was toying with these babies. Suddenly they all began wiggling. Each one making furious little fists."

The gunwoman demonstrates.

"I looked down," she says. "and caught Avadoot going blank. At that moment, all the other babies began howling! Every one — a full chorus of *whah!* "

"At high C pitch?" Clare asks, sounding professionally polite, Dix's hand still doing *wiggle, wiggle.*

"Probably," the gunwoman responds. "I, of course, knew nothing about a baby's crying back then, but even a barkeep with a tin ear could distinguish those different intonations of howling."

"You had traditional sobbing, screaming on exhalation?" Clare inquires. *Wiggle, wiggle.*

"Yup."

"Air-sucking?"

"Yup," Keegan responds.

"Cresting-whimpers?"

The gunwoman nods. "Even a pair of straight-out gutturals." She licks her lips. "But then, after some momentary fluctuation, every baby synchronized into a single cry. Each one inhaled at the same moment. The babies matched each other tone for tone, sob for sob. Just imagine the tempest! The mothers and the nurses were now the ones who got stupid — stupid with fear."

"How about you?" Clare asks, jiggling Dix's paw as if she's trying to hypnotize us.

"I wasn't afraid," Keegan says. She sounds emphatic about it. "The great Baby Combination had all the qualities of a triumph. These babies were like the Ayatollah entering Tehran. These babies were like Ronald Reagan in his fez, driving that little Shriner's car through the Houston Astrodome. These babies had just won something. Finally, the doctor rushed out of his office."

"And instantly pointed —" Clare interjects, still swaying Dix's hand, "'Ah ha. An eternal baby!'"

Keegan suddenly turns her pupils up into her head and yells, "It will be your loss for not taking me seriously, Clare."

Keegan rolls her pupils down before I can move. "I look at you and see only Sedition and Wrath. Sedition and Wrath." Keegan is pure bug eyes again. "As for Avadoot, Dr. Dewi Bhisma verified that the baby was eternal."

Who? What kind of name is that? As if she can read the mind of an angel, Keegan repeats, "Dewi Bhisma — I'll always remember the name of my first doctor. He was a Hindu. His nationality made my first M.D. both exotic and demonic." She pauses, then adds, "Probably a racist reaction."

She looks at me for confirmation. I'm standing like a Renaissance angel painting. I'm the *Annunciation*. I'm the *Adoration of the Lamb.* I give Keegan an angelic nod.

"I lied and told Bhisma the baby was mine," Keegan continues. "'How old is the baby?' he asked me, so I answered 'Ten months.' The doctor just shook his head at me and said, 'Ten months?' So I blurted out the truth."

Keegan pauses.

"I told the doctor that the baby wasn't growing. Then I confessed that I was only a nanny and had to do the mother's duty because Ms. Lindy was too much of a yuppie." The gunwoman makes her face go dead. "The doctor went white, looking like a Lost Weekend patron who suddenly drops his mug to the bar and whispers the name of his wife."

Saying that, she lets an ice cube slip out of her fingers; it slides to my feet. For no reason at all, I touch it with my toe. Cold.

"*Ah.*" Keegan sighs. "I did have an accurate eye. I later found out that Bhisma's wife was a kind of Wall Street whizzette whose friends from college had all become SoHo artists. She invested their grants for them, and they in turn bopped from party to party laughing that 'Ms. Seabrook-Bhisma is the yuppie, not us!'"

"So the doctor turned you in?" Clare asks, patting Dix's hand as if the hand is a prop.

Keegan nods. "There were phone calls to the Lindys at work. Calls put on hold. Conference calls. Threatened calls from all parties to the fuzz. Finally Gordon had to come to the doctor's office with the baby's birth certificate."

"Back up," Clare says. Wait. I notice Clare's free hand. . . .

"I don't have any sense of the Lindys. What were they like back then?"

Clare's right hand is slowly gliding on the edge of the desk.

Keegan doesn't see it. She raises her gun to her chin and says, "Thalia was never as chic as she thought she was. I used to think she was a lush, because she used Tanqueray as perfume. And she herself never saw me as anything other than a dumb Paddy."

"And Mr. Lindy?" Clare asks, her right hand moving as slowly as ice melts.

The gunwoman closes her eyes. "He was always dancing. I can see him tangoing off the elevator. Doing a two-step through the loft. Then something crazy he called *doing the yam*." She opens her eyes. "And after each nightly entrance, he'd pick up Avadoot and say something like: 'Daddy just did Fred Astaire's dig-step from *Follow the Fleet*.'"

Now the gunwoman slumps forward. "No more dancing when Bhisma took over. First the doc tried to check Avadoot into Beth Israel, but when the Lindys refused he convinced them to let him study Avadoot in the loft. Suddenly Bhisma and his crew had everything wrapped in plastic." Keegan sticks out her foot — black Chinese slipper. "We all had to wear paper shoes. While Avadoot was placed in a white crib inside a giant Plexiglas egg. The crib had numbers written on the bars — now what was that about?"

I shrug. Clare pats her prop.

"Dr. Bhisma did his doctor business for six months, but that baby stayed a baby," Keegan tells us. "Then one terrible night back home in Queens, I couldn't sleep and turned on the idiot box." She stares at Clare with eyes so dilated you could stub cigars out in them and says, "You'll never know the power television had in our lives back then. We saw Ronald Reagan getting shot. We saw the Space Shuttle explode. And I saw Dr. Bhisma reveal Avadoot's existence on a midnight talk show."

Keegan pauses and frowns at Clare's free arm, but the young nanny holds steady. The gunwoman sighs. Continues her yack: "The doc announced to the viewing public that a certain Baby X wasn't aging. He mused that Baby X was perhaps the key to 'eternal youth.' When he said that, I grabbed the phone. I had to alert the Lindys. But what if one of the nurses answered? I whipped on a dress and took a zombie train into SoHo."

Keegan pauses and stares at her Colt. "I was not alone on that train. I brought something with me. I felt the Lindys needed protection." She looks up. "So I brought Father's gun."

So many stories, so many guns. I glance at Clare. Dix's hand still jiggles, while Clare's right arm is completely outstretched across the desk.

Wait. I finally get Clare. Do you? In our Radio City drama, Clare is the magician. The cardsharp. The Ms. Don't Let Your Right Hand Know What the Left Hand Is Doing. Clare has been distracting Keegan with Dix's hands while her own free arm is reaching for a drawer of the desk.

"I found three old women waiting in the foyer of the Lindys' building," Keegan is saying. "One was even clutching pliers. I knew they had come for the baby's teeth!" The gunwoman looks at me — my face this time. "Angels have teeth — what do you eat?"

I almost say, "Angel food." But stop. Angels are ironic, not witty. I love Tex-Mex, but I can't say that. Finally I mutter, "Tofu. Angels eat tofu."

Keegan makes little curlicues in the air with the barrel of her Colt. "You need teeth for that?"

Clare fires a scowl at me from the desk, almost retracting her outstretched arm as she mouths the word, *Tofu?*

"No matter," Keegan is saying. "The old women came to pry the teeth out of Avadoot's mouth. On the TV, Dr. Bhisma had postulated that the baby's teeth caused the child to stay six months old."

Keegan suddenly gives Dix's limp hand a beady eye. I shift the weight on my bare feet to distract the gunwoman from Clare's reaching and go through angelic poses.

"I shoved through them," Keegan says, successfully distracted, "and was taking out my elevator key when Dr. Bhisma himself appeared. 'Continue up,' he commanded. *But how was he here? He was on TV.* Ah. The talk show was prerecorded. Upstairs we found Thalia and Gordon and Avadoot in the kitchen with packed suitcases."

Keegan uses her free arm to clutch an "air" suitcase.

"Like refugees they told us they were going 'underground,'" Keegan says. "But Bhisma said, 'You can't leave until my people get here from Washington.'" Keegan chuckles. "At that, Thalia suddenly cried out, 'Nancy coming *here?*' — Nancy as in Nancy Reagan. Thalia's tone was like: *Oh no the place is a mess!* That stopped the doc for a minute. But then he laughed, 'Oh — goodness no. The surgeon general.'"

The gunwoman duplicates his pose.

"After he said that, I found I had taken out Father's gun."

Keegan now turns to Clare.

As if to emphasize the drama of Keegan's story, the young

nanny is herself holding a gun. Not a Colt. Not a Daddy gun. But a nanny Glock.

Long silence.

Hallelujah! *Now this angel can put his pants on!*

"Where'd that come from?" Keegan asks, abruptly thrusting both her arms forward at the same moment Clare whips her single gun arm out too. Everyone freezes. The two women stand in this imitation Samurai pose — Colt to Glock — for a long, long time. I stop breathing. Realize the blood rushing in my angelic ears reminds me of a telephone ringing. An old-fashioned ring from before the Reagan era. A ring from a time before telephones beeped and chirped like techno-parakeets.

Clare moves first. She still points her Glock but drops Dix's hand to the desk with a wet thud. "Mexican standoff," she says.

Keegan is quiet a moment, then says, "So it's I shoot you but you shoot me."

Clare says nothing.

Then Keegan calls out, "I shoot Angel Dylan, you shoot me."

Clare, no response.

"You and I both shoot Angel Dylan, then you shoot yourself," Keegan suggests.

Clare smiles. "I don't think so."

"What's Mexican about this?" Keegan asks.

Clare shrugs.

I speak: "That's just the title of a bootleg Bob Dylan song he wrote for Sam Peckinpah."

The red gunwoman slants her shoulders. "Well, I didn't know about *that* music." Then she sighs at Clare. "I should have known you never cared a fig for Dix."

Clare just tightens her grip on her gun.

Keegan, with cartoon eyes, shakes her Colt at me. "Tell Clare what I did."

Fuck this angelic omnipotence. "No, you do it," I say.

She shakes the Diamondback.

I speak again. "It's more powerful coming from your lips."

The red gunwoman raises her free hand to her chest and says, "If you insist." She turns to Clare. "I shot the doctor with my father's Colt."

"How many times?" Clare asks, her interest piqued. "You'd never shot anyone before, right?"

Keegan laughs. "Oh, you nannies love gunplay stories, don't you?" She gives a thin smile and then turns her back to us. "It's far more interesting what I said before I did him."

I stand waiting for her to continue. Then, *Wait a minute.* Keegan is facing away from us. I might as well be the one high on drugs. But then I see that Clare is also just standing still, a tear running down her face.

I take a step —

"Stay where you are, Angel Dylan," Keegan commands, her back still to us. "Give Angel Dylan the Glock, Clare."

Clare just stands, then wipes her face with her sleeve and reaches out with the pistol.

I'm unsure.

Then I take a few steps and reach out. Take the pistol. And as I do, I visualize my winged brethren who always stand beside Christ during the Ascension. They always hold a spear that stretches down across the painting, piercing the belly of a little Satan who squirms at the Savior's feet. And the Devil is always a puny guy, sized like a cocker spaniel. And the angel guts him with superior detachment.

I take that stance as I grasp the Glock. I am superior and I am detached. And I have stopped breathing as I turn and pull the trigger. I'm not even sure what I'm aiming at.

And I still pull the trigger.

The trigger pulls and nothing happens. The gun doesn't even go *click.* Just nothing.

"I keep the clip locked up," Keegan says, turning around.

I'm standing with my mouth hanging open. Good-bye, Florentine Rockefeller essence. I'm just a fool — a naked one — with no bullets in my gun.

Keegan waves the pistol in an arc through the air. "You must have known it wasn't loaded from the weight, girl. I'm surprised."

"I knew right away," Clare says softly. "I was hoping there was a bullet in the chamber."

Keegan waves her hand, laughing. "You might be pure Sedition and Wrath, but you're also an Optimist! That's priceless!"

Saying that, Keegan pops another hit of American Magnetism into her yap — shakes her head, looking like she *really* has a monkey on her back. "Although the doctor was only the second mammal I ever shot," she says, giggling, "I had to tell him why I was shooting him."

Clare shakes her head, and suddenly lifts up Dix's head by her hair — the nanny's dead face and nose now inexplicably blackened like some sort of voodoo object.

Clare spits, "I hope that particular little story won't be as endless as this one, you long-winded potato-eater."

Keegan's elbow starts shaking and I see the vein on her palm start to flicker again. Oh shit! This naked angel takes a breath and raises one hand — a *halt* motion. No more Florentine gold-leaf ephemeralness. I am Medieval. Germanic. Carved of wood.

I proclaim: "KEEGAN!"

She turns.

"You will tell the story and then you will shoot," I intone. "But years from now, how will you know that Clare really believed you before she died?"

I pause. "Clare may be pure Sedition and Wrath, but how can she know that you're not a liar?"

Suddenly, I'm feeling really revved up — energetic. Forget this angel crap. I'm an actor. I'm a bigger actor than John Wilkes Booth. I'm more postmodern than Squat Theater. I'm both a bigger actor and more postmodern than Ronald Reagan. I'm an actor playing an angel.

A naked one. A naked messenger.

What an easy part! "I have always been observing you and the Lindys," I intone. "But Clare was not born forty years ago." I pause eight beats. "Clare believes my stories, but why should she believe yours?"

"Then you tell her," Keegan says.

I shake my head. "No can do."

I hear Clare take a breath, start to object, but I jerk my hand out — *Silence!* She drops Dix's head and crosses her arms — a *This better be good* gesture. I clear my throat — a loud, theatrical sound. What am I going to say? I have no idea. "Look, Kathleen Keegan. Mrs. Eddy told me to appear naked" — I give a slight wave to my angelic totality — "so Clare would believe me." I then hold a palm up to Kathleen, a *Well . . . and you?* gesture.

The gunwoman looks confused. She looks at Clare. Out of the corner of my eye, I see the younger woman shrug. No act —

Clare doesn't get me either. But that metaphysical lightbulb is clicking again, this time above Kathleen Keegan's head. This woman is not only high on a drug — she is high on God and Jesus and Mary Baker Eddy. What I am saying makes no logical sense to this old Christian Scientist, but I am not talking to her with logic. I speak to her with conviction. Using the right spin you can command a junkie to do anything. Eat dog food. Stand on his head. Jump out a window. That's right! It's not hard to make a junkie jump out a window. And it's not impossible to make a Christian Scientist get naked.

See there. Look at what she is doing! Keegan sways for a moment, then raises her right foot. She slides off her shoe with her free hand.

Ishmaels, this is my tableau now.

And this is my hope: men take off their pants one leg at a time. A man could disrobe using one hand, a gun clutched in his other. But a woman can't.

Don't get your feminist ire up! I have seen women undress. I've even seen Ishmaels undress.

I've seen Ishmaels slip out of their silk Nevermores and stand naked. And I tell you this: There isn't a woman in New York with or without a gun in her fist who can undress with one hand — not even if she wears a pair of single-zip Jane Austens.

Kathleen Keegan now reaches and begins a one-handed unbuttoning of the back of her red dress, still pointing the Colt. She looks calm, but says to Clare, "I'm a little nervous."

"I'll help you," Clare says, stepping closer.

Kathleen waves the gun. "No, that's okay."

Clare holds her hands up, palms out — the eternal *Don't lose your cool* gesture.

Keegan shimmies out of the dress. She wears a black half-slip, Eric von Stroheim whorehouse couture. Her brassiere is an old-fashioned, bullet-looking object.

"Clare is such a young girl," she says sadly as she folds the dress over a chair.

Clare shrugs and turns away.

I start to speak, but then don't. Kathleen Keegan is obviously not a young girl. For all my boasts of women undressing, I have never seen a woman over sixty without clothes. Should I expect wrinkles? Severe chic all over? Sags? I knew this woman when she was in her twenties — do I want to finally see her nude flesh forty years later?

Now the woman slides out of her slip. She drops her gun and reaches behind her back to unsnap her brassiere. *Now!* In the single moment that I leap across the room I comprehend that Kathleen Keegan's face is the only part of her that is weathered — her remaining self is lovely. I see that I am rushing toward a naked woman with a full figure. A woman's figure. Think of classic Greek statues of the female shape — images that are without age. Kathleen Keegan is womanly in a similar way. Perhaps she gets off on Teen Spirit. Perhaps many old women are classic this way.

Not that this naked old woman is just standing there. She senses my movement and automatically reaches for her gun. Clare is suddenly rushing at Keegan as well. As we both grab Keegan, she screams, "Stay back! The story's not over!"

Her gun discharges. Goes off. And there is no difference between my eardrums and this office on the seventh floor of the General Electric Building. Then the world is sucked black. No. I'm not shot — the flashlight has gone out.

At last! The cow gave up the ghost — the batteries are dead!

All three of us halt our struggling — I'm gripping Keegan's naked hip. The room is filled with panting, each of us breathing at a different tempo. Then big bang and muzzle flash. I fling myself belly-down onto the floor — I'm no target! — and hold my head. Shots. Shots. Then clicking. The gun is empty.

Keegan is now shouting, "What did I tell the doctor? What did I tell the doctor? I told him that I knew that as long as Avadoot was alive, the baby was a threat. Not to the government. Not to the yuppies. But Avadoot threatened doctors. Mrs. Eddy said we age because we see others aging, but I say we age because doctors want us to. Doctors were stockbrokers before stockbrokers were stockbrokers. Doctors encourage us to age so they can *corner the market.*"

She utters this Wall Street–speak and I get an involuntary sheldrake. It rolls into my head, images burning my retinas like emulsion on film — a movie with sound, from the old Dolby Stereo days: I see Keegan shooting the doctor in the back. Then she and the Lindys are all slipping and sliding in the blood on that SoHo loft floor forty years ago. I hear the sound of their soles squeegeeing Bhisma's blood as they skid into the elevator, then ride down to the lobby where the elderly dentists had been waiting with their pliers — but after gunshots, they've fled. And soon the Lindys leave SoHo and go underground like Lewis Carroll's Alice and Patty Hearst.

My sheldraking stops, and I wonder who cleaned up the doctor's body? The government? The Contras? Not so far-fetched. After all, Bhisma had contacted Washington. Both Nancy and

Ronnie were so old. Surely the Republicans wanted an eternal baby. I try sheldraking again, but only get white light. Wait. This is real stuff, not metaphoric illumination. This entire room is glowing. I see spent cartridges on the floor. Keegan's empty Colt. Flecks of pulped *Mr. Boston's* below the bookshelves. And a pool of light. Yes. There is a pool of light on the floor. But it's not sunlight. It's not a lantern or light from cowshit.

It's real electric stuff.

I look up from the floor. Both women — one naked, one clothed — are suddenly staring with open mouths at the ceiling. There is the source of the light.

A lightbulb.

A real one.

A real lightbulb protrudes from the ceiling. A General Electric Softwhite. I stand up under this glass egg — a talisman, an offering to the lost AC/DC. I myself have several lightbulbs stuck in my ceiling on West Forty-seventh Street. The three of us gather close under the face of raw current.

"Our prayers worked," Keegan is saying. "We've all been praying for the light to return and it has!"

She joins Clare and stands directly under the light — both women closing their eyes as if the bulb is a shower spigot drenching them in light.

"My God!" I say — no longer an angel but a cold, naked man. "Con Ed wasn't lying!"

Do you know what this means? The power company's Morphic Aberration was real. Consolidated Edison has been faithfully churning up current all these years waiting for the juice to boomerang back into our power lines and sockets — to return from wherever it had gone. Say, back from the 1960s? *Poor Bob Dylan,* I think. *Denied his juice at Newport — unplugged for good. . . .*

But Bob denied is New York exalted. Oh, forget anything dour I ever said about electricity — I give heartfelt welcome to this light!

I bend down and pick up the gun. Then I see Keegan biting her hand.

"What's wrong?" Clare asks.

"It's gone," the naked woman says, pawing the air around Clare's face — it's as if Keegan has gone blind. "Where's the AM?" she says.

At her words the room suddenly goes black. For all of us. Now comes a pop — a delicate sound, more brittle than a champagne cork. Pieces of glass sprinkle on our faces.

Oh boy! I remember that noise. I haven't heard it since I was a kid. That was the sound of a lightbulb popping. Poor, frail little bubble! I reach out for Clare. I'm suddenly afraid all this dark will suck her away. In the confused groping, Kathleen Keegan gets away from my grip. Clare grunts. The sound of running. Then Clare is leading me to the door, her hands patting the wall. Suddenly the hall fills with light.

"The juice isn't gone or going," I say. "The lightbulb just burned out."

Clare looks at me — says nothing — then looks at the light and says, "Wow."

She steps under the bulb in the hall, tilts her head back, and starts singing. Her voice is strong and sweetly harsh, almost Appalachian. *"Glow little glow worm, fly of fire / Glow like an in-can-des-cent wire / Glow for the female of the species . . ."*

She sings this song with more earthy authenticity than she did when she was stripping for the Radio City workers. Her singing is so moving that I walk up. Take her hand. And join her: *"Turn on the AC and the DC . . ."*

When the song is done, Clare pulls me toward a door, saying, "This way."

We step into a hallway. An office space. She disappears in the darkness, then a glowing wedge appears. She has another flashlight. I watch its light bob across the floor, then stop, as the nanny sets it down and begins to pick up Kathleen Keegan's scattered clothes.

Now she's folding them?

"Stop it, Clare," I say. "Let's get out of here. What if Keegan gets another gun?"

"She won't get another gun."

As Clare says that, I'm looking through a window in the hallway. I see something outside and what I see is amazing — floating in the night is a short piece of illuminated language.

A single word written in an orange glowing Geneva font. A single word bringing back so many memories — I am a boy sitting in a movie theater eating popcorn, waiting for the new Harrison Ford to start.

The floating word is: EXIT.

I press against the glass. Through the windows of a neighboring skyscraper, this naked man sees the word EXIT floating. Then I look down at the street. There are strange luminescent balls along Fifth Avenue. They are not fires or gaslights. They are pure crystal beads of brilliance. The electric streetlights are on.

"There's electric light all over the city!" I say. "God bless Con Ed!"

8 postmodern

FRED ASTAIRE, step aside! As I dance down the stairwell of the GE Building, I realize that electricity is consciousness. How could I have been so jaded about the juice? Electricity is life. Sounds corny, I know. Victor Frankenstein already told us this. The GE lightbulb man, Reddy Kilowatt too. . . .

But consciousness is mortality — it's the unconscious who live forever.

Shit! Clare and I could have been killed up there and never had this opportunity to witness the sweet return of New York's wattage.

But Keegan didn't shoot us.

And I'm still alive — dancing toward a fluorescent light buzzing at the bottom of this stairwell. Don't think I'm *nude descending a staircase.* "Put some pants on and get down to the street," Clare had commanded. I just laughed.

Put some pants on. Put some pants on. How can a woman bark that with such a deadpan?

"Aren't you coming?" I asked.

She shook her head while popping a tin of Vengeance. "There's things I have to do."

"What?"

"Dix. Keegan."

"Let Keegan go. I'll help you with Dix."

She shook her head. I looked at the tin of nanny dope and was about to suggest that she turn over a new leaf, and take different drugs. But no. Who am I to judge pharmaceutical preference?

"Can't you just let Keegan go?" I suggested.

Clare, puzzled: "I'm not going to pop her. We need to talk."

Talk? What have we been doing all night? The Big Talk.

I just looked at her and sighed. "It's just a nanny thing, right?"

Straight-faced, she replied, "Yup. A goddamn nanny thing." She waved her arm. "Go. Get out of there." She gave me a smile. "I'll meet you on the corner of Forty-seventh."

"I live just down the street."

"I'll meet you on the corner of Forty-seventh," she repeated.

How I now wish Clare were here to bathe in all this electric light. I ask you, Ishmaels, what is the most beautiful object a man or woman can look at?

The face of God?

The face of your newborn child?

Neither is as gorgeous as a glowing rod of fluorescent light. Listen to that gentle buzzing. Is any song sweeter?

I stagger to the street. God, it's chilly. Snow has dusted the tops of the railings and vent shafts.

There are people walking around too.

It's maybe four in the morning and Sixth Avenue is jumping like rush hour. Hundreds are gathering under the streetlamps — heads tilted back, mouths agape. I see furious electricity glowing in each cloud of breath.

I join them.

Here is the true drug — forget Vengeance. Forget Twenty Something. Oh, sweet electricity! We New Yorkers are like moths. If we had wings, we'd rise as one and beat our bodies against all this narcotic light.

We don't have wings, but some of us have babies. A woman with an infant shuffles in front of me down Forty-seventh. The child ignores the light and just peers at all us stoned adults. Here's a true Inside Child! I reach out and steer the baby's head up toward a streetlamp.

"There was darkness and now there's this," I say out loud. I say this to the baby. I don't usually talk to babies, but I do talk to dogs I find tethered outside restaurants. I guess talking to a baby is pretty natural. I can imagine a man and woman conversing with a single dog for the duration of a canine lifetime, but how could the Lindys talk to the same baby for forty years? Did they convince themselves the baby could follow their speech? Or after the first ten — fifteen — years, did they just stay silent? *Ah, Failure Baby strikes again,* I think. Maybe the Lindys believed it was their lack of parenting that kept the baby from discourse.

But now that the volts are back, how can anyone be a failure again?

I head down Forty-seventh, a narrow street of Hasidic diamond showrooms now lined with couples kissing. It's like old photos of

VE day. Love has returned to Manhattan! On instinct I try shel-draking the smoochers but get zip. Only faint vibes. Images. Traces of stories. Maybe sheldraking is gone for good. I look at the kissing couples and don't feel any loss.

I mean, I have Clare.

Or at least think I do. As the old 1960s song goes, *I Live on Love Street.* Isn't this a Dylan song? Probably. Every song from the 1960s is a Dylan song — his Morphic Resonance was so strong he colonized most songwriters. Right? But enough talk of pop music. I not only live on Love Street, but above the *store where the creatures meet.* I live two flights above the Gotham Book Mart, over a sign that says, WISE MEN FISH HERE. I peer into the store's window and see a man and a woman in the bookstore, kneeling at an outlet. They lick each other's fingers, then stick them into the socket.

Wow! This makes perfect sense. I now recall that years ago my father designed a suit called I Sing the Body Electric for the Florida penal system. In those days, murderers were actually *juiced* in twenty-five states — the guilty made one with the current. An adventurous prison official awarded my father a grant to design a suit that a prisoner could wear to feel less anxious as he or she was strapped into the lap of Old Sparky. Joltin' Judy. Now I realize those prisoners needed no suits. Just look at this couple as they kneel inside this *fishery* — those smiles! Electrocution must be the most joyful experience on earth.

I step into the bookstore — "May I?"

The woman nods and says, "Move over, Flip." Her companion makes room. I kneel between them and both take turns licking my finger. Then I touch the socket. At first, nothing. Then, oh yes! What a thing: the current! I am speechless. You know how certain hallucinogens make you feel like new brain lobes have been revealed — narrow little rooms have suddenly become banquet halls? The shock of electricity compacts my brain into a single atomic particle. Talk about the God within — this electrical glue is what joins and has always joined us together. My mouth is puckering open like a fish's. But I make no sounds. Music is playing inside my ears, but I can't sing right now. I tilt my head back, and my throat starts croaking. I find myself making the sound of a fluorescent light.

When I get back in my head, I find myself up in my apartment. God, what a mess. I change my clothes. My shoes. Brush my teeth. Then I go and dismantle my shrine. I need to show Clare what I store here, but I can't ask her up to this bachelored-out crib. I pack this electronic device in a suitcase. I'll show it to her at a hotel. Or her place downtown.

As for what Clare is doing, although I can't sheldrake her, she'll tell what happened: How she props Dix over her shoulder. Lugs the dead nanny up to the first abandoned floor on thirteen. Then she returns to NBC to find Keegan standing naked in the ladies room, dunking her head over and over in the sink.

"Help me detox," Keegan says, face dripping.

Clare grips the back of the woman's neck, then submerges her head in the full sink. Ten seconds go by and Keegan is struggling for air, but Clare presses harder. *I guess I should count or something,* she thinks. *One one-thousand. Two one-thousand. Three one-thousand . . .*

She hauls Keegan's head up. "How long can you be without air? Two minutes?"

Water runs down the old woman's face as she rolls up her eyes and screams, "Fame! Financial Security! Adventure! Health! Sexual Satisfaction!"

Clare dunks the woman a second time. "Yeah. Yeah. Yeah. Sedition, Heresies, Rebellion, and Wrath . . ."

Later, Keegan is getting dressed, giving Clare shy glances like a guilty dog. "Bad trip," she finally says.

Clare shrugs. "Do I look like me now?"

The older nanny nods.

Clare opens a tin of Vengeance and cuts a line with a guitar pick. "Tell me you haven't been pointing a Colt six-shot double-action Diamondback .38 Special at me all night because I need to hear the story of how Tooth Baby is forty years old."

Ms. Keegan frowns. "That *is* the story. But let me show you something."

Clare looks up as Keegan grabs a stray NBC pad from a desk and writes, *Avadhüt.* "This is how the baby's name should be written. It's a term in Sanskrit."

"Sanskrit?"

Keegan nods. "A language older than electricity. It means, *One who fell from the sky.*"

"So?"

"The time has come for Gordon to send Avadhüt back home before everything changes."

The nanny jerks up. "Back home? Kill the baby?"

Keegan nods.

Clare slaps the desk, shouting, "No!" — brief cloud of nanny dope — "I refuse that!" Clare folds her arms. "Why would the Lindys kill their baby?"

"Because of the dreams."

"What do you mean, dreams?" Clare demands.

"For a year, Gordon and Thalia have had the same dream."

"What dream?"

"They've dreamed over and over that they would walk up to the baby's crib and find a fully grown naked man crammed inside."

Clare shakes her head.

"And he's reading," Keegan says. "Reading your father's Inside Child book, of all things."

"How could anyone dream so much without electricity?"

"Obviously those weren't ordinary dreams," Keegan says, raising a finger. "Or ordinary sheldrakes. They're full-fledged omens."

"Of what?"

"That Avadhüt is preparing to make some sort of change," Keegan says. "How could the Lindys care for a forty-year-old child?"

Clare grabs Keegan's collar. "The Lindys are not going to hurt the baby."

"Please, Clare."

The young nanny doesn't let go. The drums are beginning in her head.

"Your AM," Keegan says. "It used to overpower me."

Clare's temples are banging: *Vengeance. Vengeance. Vengeance.* "I used to overpower you, great," she mutters, closing her eyes and clenching her teeth. *Shut up! Stop that goddamn drumming.*

"But now — nothing," Keegan whispers.

Clare opens her eyes. "Just shhhh, now." She lets go of Keegan's collar. A moment passes.

"How do they plan to do it?" Clare asks.

"Roman-style," Keegan says quietly.

Clare looks blank, then says, "Just leave the baby in a field?"
Keegan nods.

Clare pulls the old woman's sleeve — a movement causing
blood to rush into the young nanny's ears, a surging that reminds
her of the sweet sound of gunfire. "Come on," Clare commands.

Keegan shakes her head. "Something had to be done for the
baby eventually. What would happen to Avadhüt when Gordon
and Thalia are gone? I'm too old to care for the child." She smiles.
"And you're just a Vengeance junkie."

Clare pulls Keegan across the room. "Come on. We're going
to Jersey. To get the baby."

Ms. Keegan protests. "You don't need me."

Clare stops and kicks off her flats, muttering, "You're going
to control that old fool Lindy." Clare opens a desk drawer and
paws out a pair of Deerstalker boots.

"I'm not coming," Keegan says.

"You're coming," Clare says, putting on one boot.

"I'm not."

"If you don't, I'll shoot you and spit in the wound," Clare
snarls, putting on the other boot. Then she stands and slips a little
nanny belly gun in her waistband. Sticks a larger revolver in her
pocket. "I'll smoke anyone who fucks with the Lindys' beautiful
baby. Understand?"

"Kill them all and let Mary Baker Eddy sort them out," Keegan says, straight-faced.

Clare looks blank.

"I made a joke," Keegan says.

"Let's go." Clare shoves the old woman toward the door.

• • •

Clare and Keegan leave Radio City about the same time that I'm walking back toward Sixth Avenue with my suitcase. And it's here on Forty-seventh Street that I hear it: a delicate sound accompanying all these pedestrians standing in doorways kissing. It's a Christmasy sound — a petite Salvation Army cowbell. Pucker your lips and go, *Brrring. Brrring.* That's the sound of a ringing telephone. I was historically inaccurate when I said earlier that phones chirped like techno-parakeets during the Reagan era.

Pay phones didn't.

And it's a pay phone that's ringing now. There at the curb. It's a real Ma Bell, not some cheap deregulation knockoff. Most of you have read how pay phones worked, so I don't have to stress that they weren't always adorned with sticks of incense and tin amulets of saints. Maybe it's a saint who's ringing right now to congratulate me on my earlier performance as an angel. I reach out and paw away the flowers and shrine ornaments. Goddammit, someone has lashed the receiver to the hook with a rosary. As I untie the thing a woman barks behind me, "Hands off, pin-dick."

I spin around.

"This call is mine."

I get an instant dose of mammal claustrophobia! A huge horse stands behind me on the sidewalk. Big brown flank. Navaho saddle blanket. Woman rider towering above me. She opens her riding jacket to show me the pistols strapped to her billowy pink tunic.

"Give it to me or I'll shoot your nuts off," she spits from her perch.

She's a nanny, of course. But get her outfit! What is it? It's definitely Lit Wear, but looks French.

I hand her the receiver.

Wait. I recognize her blouse. God. Love has truly returned

to Manhattan when a gun-toting nanny is decked out in a Madame Bovary.

She lifts the phone to her ear. Listens a moment. Then starts snapping, "You sure? You sure?"

I look past her beast and see that the middle of Forty-seventh Street is full of horses, a cavalry that's a cross between The Book of Revelations horsemen and Flaubert. Dozens of women sit astride ponies and mares, belts of ammo wrapped bandit-style across the bodices of their Madame Bovarys.

"If you're shittin' us, we'll gut-shoot you seven times from Tuesday and spit in the wounds," the nanny screams above me. (I later learn the reference to spitting is a standard nanny epithet.) Then she flings down the receiver.

"Hang it up," she commands, already turning in her saddle. "Let's ride, girls," she yells.

The horses start snorting and the nannies ride past me down the street, heading east. I see they're an old crew — many of the riders are Keegan's age. Or even older, like mummies who have ridden out of some ancient Egyptian exhibit uptown at the Met. But then I also see young ones. Some I even recognize from Washington Square Park.

There's Raven Beak. George Washington Jaw. Those NBC nannies are no longer decked in Poe or Bierce, but costumed in Bovarys like the others. Wait a minute! Oh no! Has this Flaubert cavalry come to avenge Dix?

I run after them. I won't let Clare be caught in any crossfire — not that I have a clue how to stop them. But then maybe I won't have to. At Sixth Avenue, the nannies keep riding east, weaving their horses around kissing couples. Oh my God, are these equine nannies from hell just out riding for amour? God save any love objects they round up. . . .

• • • •

I cool my heels on the corner of Forty-seventh for ten minutes, then Clare and Keegan show up — the young nanny with one hand jammed in her coat, the other gripping Keegan's sleeve.

"Am I glad you're okay," I say. "I just saw your compatriots —"

"Shut up," Clare spits through gritted teeth. "I'm thinking."

Keegan gives me a shrug. Then asks, "Who are you, then, if not an angel?"

I start to speak. Then don't. Then say, "Just think of me as the ghost of electricity until you remember who I am."

"Come on, you two," Clare orders. "We're going to Jersey."

A block later, Clare says, "Sorry I snapped at you. What's in the suitcase?"

"I'll show you later," this ghost says.

Clare turns away.

"I'm still assuming that you're not really a Christian Science angel," Keegan says.

"Not the last time I checked," I tell her.

"Aren't you surprised by the cold?" Keegan asks, looking around at the kissing couples. "Did the electricity cause this freezing?"

Now I'm the one shrugging. "The smooching certainly didn't."

Clare hurries us to Broadway, but we find the Times Square river-to-river Trot Lines aren't running — everyone is too excited about the returning watts.

"It will take forever if we walk," Clare complains.

"What else can we do?" (At heart I'm a stoic.)

We walk west. The sky gets brighter. At the river, a ferry bobs beside the pier. Empty.

Clare: "Damn. They've shut it down."

Keegan: "Look, there's the skipper!"

I can see a guy in a captain's hat slouching in a lifeboat, smoking. "Ah, finally. Some customers!" he says as we hurry aboard. "Why is everybody making such a big deal about the return of electricity? It's like they're looking forward to getting bills from Count Con Ed once a month."

Clare shrugs and shows him her Glock. "Get this tub floating," she commands. "Now."

On the float across the Hudson, I just stare at the sky. No carrier pigeons today. No messages. No words.

"There's no reason to be sailing to New Jersey," Keegan complains. "We're too late."

"Shut up," Clare mutters.

"Too bad you were never one of those modern quantum girls," Keegan says to the younger nanny. "Then you'd understand what happened."

Clare says nothing.

"Don't you see the Lindy baby was the Morphic Abbreviation —"

"Aberration," I say.

The old woman looks puzzled.

"Morphic Aberration." I repeat.

"Whatever," Keegan says, dismissing me. "What I mean to say is the Lindy baby was responsible for the disappearance of electricity. Now that the power is back, we know the baby is gone."

Clare snaps out her arm and grabs Keegan's collar. "The Lindys' baby has nothing to do with the disappearance and return of electricity. We are going to get to Jersey in time."

Keegan continues peering into Clare's eyes.

"Now what?" the young nanny sighs.

"Your eyes are so glassy," Keegan says. "I'm responsible for your addiction, aren't I."

Clare gives a bitter laugh and sings, "Oh, you old pusher, you gave me the Vengeance habit bad."

We just float some more in silence — me straddling my suitcase with my feet. Clare suddenly takes a step forward and jerks my head down to her mouth. And bites my lip.

I cry out and back away.

"It's a Vengeance thing," she laughs. "Here's to the return of electricity and love."

There's blood in my mouth. I have nothing to say to that, but I'm grinning.

Clare turns to Keegan. "How did the Lindys end up in California?"

"Thalia quit her job," Keegan says, "and Gordon got Ozu to transfer him to the L.A. office. Out in California, the Lindys just moved from apartment to apartment so no one could get suspicious about their permanent baby. Whenever Gordon had to produce a son for a company function, he hired a child actor named Dylan to fly out and play the part, since he was the same calendar age as Avadoot."

She pauses. "And of course that other Dylan was aging as a normal child," she adds.

Doesn't she recognize me yet?

"But then, that particular Dylan has been dead for years and years," Keegan says.

Oh really?

"I heard he died back when Los Angeles sank into the Pacific."

How does that Bob Dylan song go — *Reports* [breath] *of my death* [breath] *were greatly exaggerated?*

And since I've now become the Ghost of Electricity for real, let me be the one to tell you about California. Didn't I promise you that I would alert you when I was going to tell the truth? That moment could be now. I know about Soda, and I've always known about Avadhüt. I just couldn't believe that they were the same baby. Let me tell you again about flying in the middle of the night to Los Angeles. God, in those days none of us knew that electricity had already started to disappear. That it was happening below us. In the trenches of the Pacific, electric fish and lantern eels were dying, their bodies floating to the surface forming massive islands of phosphorescence where cargo ships would be marooned on their way to Indonesia. When the volts started dying on the islands, no one ever imagined it was permanent. We thought the great West Coast brownout was just because of earthquake weather. In our ease and ignorance we still flew in airplanes and watched movies. And even slept. Inside the particular TWA that I was flying aboard, I still possessed more than enough personal kilowatts to dream. I myself could have dreamed all night, but I was too keyed to be sleepy. L.A. always jacked me up with anticipation. I just wandered the aisles, peering into each flyer's slack mouth. I remember that the sun wasn't even up when we landed. These flights were called *red-eyes,* but I saw no bloodshot eyes as I stepped off the plane. By the tarmac, a woman grabbed my arm. "Dylan," she said.

At last, someone recognized me from my movies! But no. It was Thalia Lindy

"I'm Thalia Lindy," the woman said. "Remember me?"

I shrugged. But I did remember her. I had portrayed her son four times previously — two in New York, the rest out here. I played the kid as a toddler. First grader. Cub Scout. I never met the kid I was impersonating, but I assumed he was my age — there was just something about him they were keeping from Mr. Lindy's Japanese employers. I wasn't curious what that something was, mind you. I was twelve years old. I was only curious about myself.

Thalia Lindy gave me a long yawn. "Let's take a ride. I'll show you something wonderful."

We drove the freeway from the airport out east into the Mojave scrub. It was seven in the morning and I wanted breakfast, but this woman was intent on showing me what turned out to be a roadside attraction: two giant concrete buildings built in the shape of a brontosaurus and a tyrannosaurus rex. The dinosaurs seemed *cheesy*. The rex's white teeth looked cool, but that was it. As a man I have returned to these buildings and appreciate their weathered charm, but to a boy they were low-rent — certainly not high-tech like the robotic/Jurassic perfection of Disneyland.

"Let's go inside," the Lindy woman said.

"No," I pouted. "No way."

"Oh, come on, Dylan. You want to. Come on."

"I want some breakfast."

"You can get breakfast after the dinosaurs."

"I want breakfast now."

"You can get breakfast in the dinosaurs."

"No you can't."

"Look! Over there! That man is eating an ice cream cone. I bet your mother never let you have ice cream for breakfast."

"I want pancakes."

"You're just saying that because you think I'll tell your mother that you had ice cream for breakfast. But I'm not your mother. I won't say a word. It will be our Good Humor secret."

"No," I whined.

In my brief career between *Son from Mars* and *The Man Who Respected Women,* I had stood up to several notoriously difficult actresses. The boy I was assumed Thalia Lindy would be child's play.

She left the car and went into the concession stand and came back with two ice cream cones. The boy that I was would have loved an ice cream breakfast if she had brought back chocolate or peanut butter. Something brown. Maybe even strawberry. But she was carrying two cones with single scoops of green. Men favor this flavor, but we all know boys won't eat pistachio. Boys won't eat anything that is green because green is the color of broccoli and asparagus.

The boy that I was crossed his arms and said, "No!"

Thalia Lindy left the car again and disappeared into the stand. A long moment later, she used her butt to back out the doors holding two cardboard trays.

Oh boy! I thought. *She got one of every flavor!*

I was going to have fun.

But she hadn't.

She was carrying two trays of — twenty? thirty? — green ice cream cones. She headed back to the car. I should tell you that this car was white. The Lindy woman began sticking the green cones upside down on the hood. Then she went to the trunk. A moment later, there were light thumps on the roof.

Then she got in behind the wheel. "Now we're a dinosaur," she said.

It made sense in a crazy kind of way. Her car was a stegosaurus. The woman's craziness was both novel and manageable. Ms.

Lindy had always seemed a typical high-strung professional wife/ mother when I played her kid before. I'd once been on a movie set when a notoriously difficult actress smeared a costar's penis with Krazy Glue, so ice cream on a car wasn't anything I couldn't handle. A stream of green pistachio began dripping down the windshield. Thalia Lindy backed out of the parking lot.

"Where are we going?" I asked.

No answer.

Most of the cones stayed stuck to the car, and green streams ran across the hood.

Thalia Lindy bit her lip and suddenly swung us over to a blacktop road that ran parallel to the highway, singing, "I am the Road Warrior!"

Her voice was terrible.

The woman looked at me and yelled, "No, that's not it. What I am is the Inside Child."

I pointed out the window, but she refused to watch the road.

"My father would never let me sing," she told me. "He conducted the Palatine Methodist choir and he wouldn't let me sing — but my Inside Child is singing now —"

Then she gave a long shrill cry of "*Ahrooo!*"

I reached for the wheel. But her grip was stronger. In our brief struggle, the wipers got switched on — smearing the whole windshield with a green sheen. We were driving underwater. The Lindy woman laughed and began watching the road. "You know what? My Inside Child is a brat!" She laughed and started pounding the horn.

The woman missed the freeway ramp and swung wide for the underpass, lead-footing us down a narrow road straight into the wasteland. We drove in silence until the engine began backfiring. The tailpipe banged for a few minutes, then the whole car shuddered and rolled to a stop.

"Damn. Empty," she said.

We sat for a while. The ice cream cones had long since rolled off the hood, leaving the metal glistening with sticky green. She turned and gave me a steady look. "Do you remember Avadoot — my baby?"

I shook my head no. I really didn't.

"You're the same age as Avadoot."

So what? I didn't say anything.

"I'd like to burp you," she said, adding, "that is, when you need to be burped."

What was she talking about?

She touched my arm. "Will you let me burp you sometime, Dylan?"

I had no idea what she meant, so I yanked open the door and jumped out and ran from the car. The air was like hot breath only drier. I ran up a hill and waited behind a Joshua tree. The car just sat. I expected it to drive away, but nothing happened. Then a camper passed. Stopped. Backed up. An old guy with silver hair got out and walked to the Lindy car, eyes fixed on the single cone still stuck on the trunk. He stared at it a long time before Thalia Lindy lowered her window. The two spoke. Then he walked to the hood and opened it. He fiddled with the engine. He walked to his camper and returned with a portable phone — Alexander Graham Bell even out here in the desert! I watched the woman make a call. Boy, did she talk. I turned and wandered into the scrub. I came upon a scattering of picnic tables, where I was recognized by some hikers. Finally! They turned out to be big *Son from Mars* freaks. They offered to share their pita sandwiches and later we all posed together in front of a Polaroid camera with a timer. None of them asked for my autograph — I was bummed. It wasn't until years later that it dawned on me that they were *Logos No!* fanatics.

The day was burning, so I walked back to my hill. Now a black sedan was parked behind Thalia's car, and I recognized Gordon Lindy filling her tank from a gas can. He'd lost a lot of hair but had the same thin build that I remembered. Then I saw a baby strapped in an infant car seat beside Ms. Lindy. Her husband stopped pouring, knocked three times on the trunk. The car started — the tailpipe coughed — then Thalia Lindy gunned the car down the road. Lindy had noticed me. I turned my eyes away. "Gordon Lindy," he said a moment later, out of breath, "Remember me?"

"Sure." I said. "My father."

He had extended his hand. As I reached to shake it, he gripped my wrist and led me down the hill. "She freaked you out, huh?" he asked as we picked our way down over the rocks. I nodded. He still had my hand.

"You must be thirsty. I've got some soda in the car." Then he started laughing. He stopped and was pointing into the distance. "See those mountains?"

I did. *So what?*

"The Soda Mountains," he said. Then he added, "That's what they're named."

So what? I thought. *They could be called Coca-Cola Ridge, big deal. . . .*

The inside of his car smelled of talcum powder. Mr. Lindy sat behind the wheel with his eyes shut, pinching the bridge of his nose for a long time before he drove us out of the desert.

Mr. Lindy had me camped out at the Raceda Holiday Inn. I shrugged off my encounter with the Lindy woman, stayed up all night scarfing Baby Ruths and scanning the TV for the dozen or so commercials I had once appeared in. I awoke to a screen full of static and Kathleen Keegan shaking my shoulder — my handler when I impersonated Lindy's kid.

"Rise and shine, Rasputin, Jr.," she sang, leaning over the bed. "And everyone says that Dustin Hoffman is difficult."

I smiled. It had been four years since this actor had seen this woman last. She glanced away from me for a moment and I was staring down her blouse. Kathleen wasn't wearing a brassiere. I had never looked down this woman's blouse when I was three, let alone four or five. But this Dylan was no longer a boy.

"Well, say something," she said.

"It's great to see you, Kathy! Let's go to Malibu."

She stood. "You haven't reached sufficient social elevation, let alone maturity, that you can call me Kathy. Because you are an old associate, you may refer to me as Kathleen in private, but I insist on being Ms. Keegan in public."

I shifted on the bed so I could look down her blouse again.

"Mr. Lindy told me that you were pulling a DeNiro," she told me. "I'm here to yank you in line." She gave a brief smile. "And from this moment onward, stop looking down my blouse."

· · ·

Mr. Lindy drove Kathleen and me to Echo Park.

"Dodger Stadium is just over that foothill," he told me.

I shrugged.

The Lindys lived in a stucco bungalow. Thalia Lindy was at the door and immediately started yapping at her husband — "What we're doing is not right. Let's just tell Ozu about our Inside Child!"

Oh, she's still crazy . . .

Gordon Lindy took his wife's arm and ushered her into the dim house. Kathleen and I followed, and stood in the living room while the Lindys squabbled. As much as I could make out, Thalia Lindy wanted to cancel my performance.

"Don't worry, Dylan," Kathleen said. "Thalia hasn't gone that cuckoo."

Then the doorbell rang. Mr. Lindy came and looked out through the curtains.

"Shit."

He said "Shit" a second time, then, "It's Nixon."

Oh wow! The Watergate guy here?

Mr. Lindy rushed toward Kathleen, exclaiming, "Hide Dylan."

Kathleen led me into a room and shut the door — then leaned hard against it as if she expected someone to try to get in.

I whispered, "What's Richard Nixon doing here?"

"What?"

I pointed. "Nixon — at the door."

"No no no," she said. "It's a different one. Someone from Ozu. Just keep quiet."

"What's Ozu?"

"A Greek wine," she said, and put her hand over my mouth.

I twisted out of her grip. The room was small and only contained a dog basket and a crib. I didn't know the Lindys had a dog. I noticed that the crib was covered with strange designs. I went closer. They appeared to be leaping rabbits but looked a little crazy. The man (or angel) I now am, thirty years later, can describe them as *Picassoesque* — profile and portrait becoming one. The boy that I was stood examining the crib rabbits so closely that he didn't immediately register the small body inside, facing the wall.

"Dylan, no!" Kathleen hissed.

I paid her no mind and saw the baby. As I told you, I knew the Lindys had a kid my age, but I never knew they had a baby. Then this baby — whomever it belonged to — turned. It moved slowly, leisurely even. To peer at me with a blank face. I didn't think, *Oh boy, an eternal baby!* This baby did seem familiar, however. And I looked over my shoulder to ask Kathleen why. But there were voices near the door, and she swatted me silent. When I looked back into the crib, I met the stare of a baby absolutely seething with disdain. This look was somehow familiar. A therapist would lean back in his chair and say, "Where have you seen a look like this before?" I would answer, "Perhaps we passed each other as babies as we were being wheeled through the streets of SoHo in our buggies and the Lindy child shot me a similar glare of contempt — that's what I was remembering." The therapist would nod, then ask, "Did your mother ever look at you like that?" *Oh. Right. Everything must lead back to Mom. God, therapy drives me nuts.* I don't know why the baby stared at me that way, but Young Dylan knew he was not going to be evaluated — *put down* — by a baby. He was almost a man. He owned a razor. He used shaving cream. So I stood my ground. Me and the baby tried to pin each other with our eyes. I certainly felt nothing resembling Clare's Cone Heart. I felt the steely rage of the sumo wrestler before he bumps bellies.

Then the baby reached out with one little hand.

I put my own hand between the bars of the crib, index finger extended. I could tell the therapist that this was the way I held my hand and offered my finger to Harrison Ford's pet monkey.

Little pet monkey. Little pet baby. Who had contempt now? Surely in the aikido of contempt, Young Dylan had achieved the black belt!

Our fingers touched. Several pages back, I told you how the socket at the Gotham Book Mart felt. I recall that the baby's touch was similar. But not quite the same. The baby's electricity wasn't so overt: I didn't shout and pull my finger away. I would look at that finger later and not see a singe or a mark. I'm sure that this was not Cone Heart. It was more like the spark of a thought went from the baby to me. My finger was the plug. The baby, the socket. I found myself thinking, *I'm not old enough to understand this.* But the next second, Young Dylan decided, *I am fucking well old enough.* Old enough for everything. I even looked down women's blouses. I knew what I was doing. Suddenly Kathleen was over me. "Come away, Dylan. Come away from the baby."

I turned. She was leaning forward, and I craned my neck and looked. I wasn't exactly sure what a man did after he finished looking — but I knew this peering down a woman's blouse was a cool and manly thing. My gaze hadn't changed since that morning, but I had an inkling of something I wanted. I looked at Kathleen's breasts and said, "I'm hungry, Kaffleen, feed me."

She was kind and just led me away from the baby.

That powerful, powerful baby.

The next thing I remember is the banquet. I have no idea what happened between getting zapped by the baby and being surrounded by those hundreds of smiling Asians, each pinching a cocktail glass. Many had poodles, and these dogs gave little yips. TechnoPop music played. We were at the Château Marmont. Recognize the name? Now and then, I meet an Ishmael who's never heard of the place — if that's you, know that this hotel was as French as the old Garden of Allah was Moroccan.

I was tagging behind Mr. Lindy and Kathleen. Ms. Lindy had been left behind in Echo Park with the baby. Kathleen was impersonating Lindy's Irish wife on the assumption that someone had to keep an eye on my performance. But I knew the real reason she was here was that Mr. Lindy's wife had become too California to be trusted — her husband had eighty-sixed her from the ball.

Various Japanese men walked up to Lindy saying, "Good move getting these festivities transferred to L.A."

If any of them addressed me, I just mumbled the lines Lindy taught me. "I want to be a digital technician like my father before me."

I was struck with the thought that it was to be nothing but corporate imitation gigs from here on out. There would be no *Son from Mars II*. No *Men Who Respected Women*. I realized that back in Echo Park that baby had condemned me to obscurity. There I was, a has-been, still too young for whiskey or suicide. Then Thalia Lindy appeared and presented that terrible baby who had done this to me.

Yes!

The woman pushed her way through the crowd until she reached the middle of the room. Then she carefully lifted the baby high above her head, turning slowly for all to see. "This is Gordon Lindy's true child!" Thalia Lindy yelled.

The Lindy baby looked at the crowd from the air. I immediately looked down. Then was ashamed at myself for being chicken. I looked back. The baby was scanning us all without scorn or judgment. The baby looked as if it belonged above our heads. Many forks froze. Drinks paused in mid-sip. The baby controlled everyone's eating.

"This is our real child — my real baby," Thalia shouted. "And my baby has been a baby for twelve years. But this will all change. I used to think that my baby had stayed this way because my husband and I were selfish yuppies, but selfish behavior is not bad. You Japanese know better than anyone that selfishness is only a symptom of a higher state. Selfishness is just love — love directed at yourself. . . . And if you yourself aren't selfish, how could anyone else love you? Being born is selfish. Being a baby is selfish. We were conceived and born selfish and all our mothers loved us for it! I realized how much I've ignored myself. I've ignored my feelings. I ignored my own Inside Child. I suddenly realized that this baby is the physical manifestation of my Inside Child. Oh! My psyche spewed my Inside Child out into the world!"

She did a slow spin with the baby held above her head. The baby who had showed such contempt for me now had a calm, regal expression. Whether that baby was the Inside Child or not, that child was divinity that wanted worship. Several caterers began crossing themselves.

"My husband and I have finally learned to accept that our child is the Inside Child," Thalia Lindy shouted. "And we must nurture ourselves so that our baby can transform into a flesh-and-blood child, and finally, finally, finally grow up!" She paused and one by one looked her audience in the eye. "This must sound crazy to you, I know. But it is the truth. Crazy truth!" She made a small spin again — this time showing the baby to the crowd in the back of the room.

"I understood about the Inside Child long ago, but my husband only comprehended it yesterday. In a desert. With a range of mountains in the distance. I suddenly realized that we must rename our baby. Why should we be bound by the name we chose twelve years ago when we were ignorant that our baby was our Inside Child! The mountains in the desert were the Soda Mountains. And in honor of that terrain, our baby will take that name. Soda Lindy may have been an Avadhüt from the sky, but now our child will tower above us like mountains."

At those words, the baby eyed me. And I was struck by the authority of failure. By that, I had the sense that I could strive to achieve great things and fail, but my failure would be noble. Even hip. Then the baby laughed. The baby laughed and laughed and laughed. And I knew the baby had now denied me even this. It came to me that this terrible baby was as sentimental as God had been when he created the world.

Surely I was the only one affected by the baby this way. The general buzz in the Marmont was *This woman's husband should control his wife.* This woman's husband was in fact translating his wife's speech for the Ozu Shogun — "She is now talking about how wonderful babies of all nations are," Gordon was saying. "And how wonderful it is that Japanese cars are now being built to protect them —" With a choke, Mr. Lindy suddenly stopped talking and started crying.

"What's wrong?" the Shogun asked, using perfect English.

Mr. Lindy looked over in amazement. "You understand?"

The Shogun didn't say anything.

Lindy moved his lips back and forth. Finally he said, "Oh shit. All those meetings and you've always understood."

The Shogun nodded.

Mr. Lindy started speaking. "You won't be able to believe this, but what my wife said is true. Our baby has been a baby for the past twelve years. Our baby can't walk. Can't talk. Our baby is not physically growing. Worse, our baby still has the mind of an infant. My child can gaze at the bunnies on his crib for hours." He took the Shogun's arm. "Sometimes Thalia and I have conversations with our baby as if the thing were only a figment of our imagination." He closed his eyes and shook his head. "You know, I used to dance for my baby. I'd dance like Fred Astaire. Now I can't. I haven't danced in years."

"Dance?" the Shogun asked.

"Yes, dance," Mr. Lindy said. "Our baby is the same age as Fred Astaire was when he danced with his sister Adele. When Fred was twelve he was dancing onstage — my child can't even crawl!"

"Dance for me," the Shogun commanded. "Dance for me, Gordon."

Mr. Lindy was surprised. He stood very still — for a long time. Then he fumbled a bit. These were the wrong shoes, but he put a tentative foot forward. He began tapping it, searching for a beat. Then he heard something — distant music inside him. He began shuffling his feet. He began muttering, "Let's cut the rug. Ball the jack. Hoof it. Kick!"

The Shogun watched. He smiled and asked, "Isn't this what you've always wanted to do?

Mr. Lindy stopped. "Yes. I want to be a dancer."

He got quiet for a moment. "I'm too old to go onstage professionally. But I could teach it. I could teach it swell!" He smiled when he realized that he said *swell* like he was Mickey Rooney talking to Judy Garland.

The Ozu Shogun said, "I believe you are a good man. Do these things." He touched Gordon on the shoulder, a tender touch, but a touch that meant the Japanese man was going to move on to someone else. Gordon kept talking about how he wanted to leave L.A. and go home to New York. He told of other things he wanted. The Shogun frowned: Lindy was proving to be just another greedy American — *gimmie gimmie gimmie* . . .

Kathleen Keegan has been telling her version of California — a narration not much different than mine. "Gordon was transformed when we returned to New York," she insists, grabbing the Clare gun arm. "He's the one who backed the Nanny Broker Company so I could provide them with a new nanny every six months. That way no one would suspect their baby was staying a baby. We'd given up thinking Avadhüt would ever age. Instead, we all lived as anonymously as possible. And when the electricity went, it didn't faze us much because of that anonymity. Thalia had her singing while Gordon had his soft shoe. I guess that I became the adventurous one, as I was the first New Yorker to realize that nannies should take narcotics and carry guns."

Clare starts to say something, then doesn't.

"Because the electricity went, NBC flourished," Keegan says.

Clare's face is flush as she grinds her teeth. *Vengeance. Vengeance. Vengeance.*

•   •   •

We dock. It's around noon. Things seem a little out of whack here on the Jersey side. There are a few power lines down. On the horizon, smoking houses.

"The wires must have overloaded," I say.

"What does that mean?" Clare asks me.

I start to explain the mechanics of electrical production but realize that neither woman is paying attention. They're looking at one lone figure sitting under the Reagan Mon — the girl Clare stole the slingbacks from.

The Cone Heart girl.

She hunches forward, rubbing her bare feet on the frozen ground, clutching a pair of cheap Mary Janes. Clare runs over and without a word yanks off both her Deerstalkers and sets them down beside the girl. *Poor little blue toes!* Clare kneels and rubs the girl's feet.

I walk up with my suitcase as the girl tries to talk, only her teeth are chattering too much. It's all she can do to jabber out, "I can't fe-fe-feel your hands!"

Clare begins sliding the girl's numb feet into the Deerstalkers.

"No. No. No," the girl says, shaking her head. "I really need a baby."

Clare stands up and looks at the girl's feet. "You're about ten minutes from frostbite."

Not to mention that you'll never be able to stomp wine, I think. Clare turns away. Shrugs. Puts her Deerstalkers back on.

I wonder if Keegan has run away, but she's waiting for us a block from Big Pink. As we all walk to the Lindy's, Clare slips a pinch of Vengeance in her cheek. I grip my suitcase tighter and glance at the sky, where a single bird is flying. One lone, lost message. We all pause on Lindy's pink porch, watching the bird.

Clare says, "We're not late," with determination.

Kathleen Keegan gives a sad smile and opens the door. We all enter the foyer. Big Pink is cold. Quiet.

"Gordon! Thalia!" Keegan calls. Her voice is shaky.

Silence. I try a habitual sheldrake but get a big zero. I put my suitcase down near the door and search the house. There's nothing amiss in the living room. Nothing in the kitchen. Then there's music. A piano. A tango or something — coming from Jersey Bounce Studio.

"Stay here," Clare says, drawing her gun. She heads through the storeroom, the upstairs dwarf dragging something above her head. I follow. I note the veins on her temples pounding, *Vengeance. Vengeance.* We go through the courtyard toward the dance room, where someone — the Japanese accompanist? — is pounding the ivory.

Clare holds her hand to my chest and opens the door herself. I can't see inside, but hear the piano.

"Caesar!" Clare calls.

Suddenly a male voice sings, *"Howard just pointed with his gun, and said, 'That way down Highway Sixty-one.'"*

Howard just pointed with his gun? Something is wrong. Clare runs by me, slips back in the house. I look into the piano room. There's no one there. . . . Where did Caesar go?

I go into the house, the limping dwarf following above my head. I see Keegan standing frozen by the Lindy's bedroom door. I look in. I see Clare. There are dozens of bonding mobiles hanging from the ceiling room — forty years of Lindy faces. Below, two bloody bodies.

In the electric days, I saw plenty of splatter films. But that was twenty years ago. I have no context for this carnage.

Mr. Lindy lies on his bed, still clutching a pair of shoes. Mrs. Lindy is shoved between the bed and the wall.

"Gordon. Gordon. Gordon." Keegan starts wailing from the doorway.

Clare turns to me. Her face is cold. "Nannies did this," she says. "A talk job — done professionally but with a little too much gusto."

I can feel my face scrunch up. "What's a talk job?"

"The Lindys were supposed to tell someone something," Clare says.

Now Keegan is in the middle of the room, making choking sounds. "It was all for nothing. All for nothing. The baby is gone, and Gordon is dead."

"Get out," Clare says softly.

Keegan reaches out and touches the wall as if she's trying to get her balance. She closes her eyes and shakes her head.

Clare looks once more around the room. "Where is the baby?" Then she runs into the nursery. I follow. Empty. But someone has scratched the middle bunny — a downward curve cut on his face. This bunny is frowning.

We return to the bedroom and find Kathleen gripping a wet cloth, washing Gordon's face.

"We have to find the baby," Clare says.

Kathleen looks up. "The baby?" Then she fingers Gordon's forehead and starts laughing. "Gordon's baby? I loved being with him so much. I loved him."

Clare walks up. "Kathleen — forget about Gordon. Gordon is here. The baby isn't. Where is the baby?"

Kathleen looks away. "Last night Gordon told me that he knew what the secret of Avadhüt was. He knew when Avadhüt had been conceived and why Avadhüt would never grow up."

Clare interrupts. "Where is the baby? I'm not listening to any more stories — where is that lovely little baby?"

Keegan raises her eyes. "Did you hear what you just said?"

Clare gives a kerosene laugh.

"You see, Avadhüt is more than a lovely little baby," Keegan insists. "More than an eternal baby. He is the Baby of Our Age."

Clare just rolls her eyes.

"Yes. It's how the child was conceived," Keegan says, grabbing Clare's arm. "In 1981. For more than a year, Gordon told me, he and Thalia had been trying to get her pregnant. But it wasn't working. Gordon knew the problem was all his — deep in his heart he didn't feel worthy to conceive a child. Then one morning, he awoke hormonally sanctified, envisioning himself as a William Blake drawing of Jehovah. Thalia had already left for work, so Gordon rendezvoused with her at her office. He had his way with her in the elevator. He pushed the Pause button and turned his wife against the wall and entered her there between the twenty-second and twenty-first floors. And when they finished and the door slid open, the husband and wife stepped out into a lobby filled with a small crowd gathered around the guard's desk. And they were watching TV. Mr. Lindy's first thought was: *There's a camera in the elevator. They saw us on closed circuit!* Then they learned Ronald Reagan had been shot. Just five minutes before. Mr. Lindy realized that the moment those bullets had been pumped into the old man's chest, he — a young man of thirty-one — had been pumping life into his wife."

Keegan waits for a response. What can we say?

"It was during that Reagan-gunned-down moment they conceived their child," she insists. "And to Gordon's mind, that made their baby the Baby of Our Age."

And then we hear it. The song of our age: crying. A distant baby crying. Crying calmly.

"Wow," Clare says. "Listen!"

The two women both hold their heads like dogs.

"No panicked abandonment wails," Clare says. "No complaint about poop-in-diapers."

"It's just the cry of a baby coming to terms with cause and effect," Keegan whispers. "A baby who knows that crying will make food appear."

"Maybe the baby is giving signals so he can be found," I suggest.

Clare pinches my cheek. "Bright guy." Then she's holding her small belly gun in one fist while handing Keegan a Glock with the other. "The killers may be out there."

"So modern," the old Christian Scientist junkie says, fingering the pistol.

"You stay here," Clare says to me.

I stand there in the bedroom, looking out the door. Then I hear something behind me and turn. I told you Dix's wound reminded me of a chrysanthemum. Well, there is nothing floral about this old man's wounds, but suddenly his eyes open. Wide. He's moving his lips. I run over to him. The man has metamorphosed completely into the figure from *American Gothic.*

"I'm dying," he says. Then gives a weak laugh. "What an obvious thing to say."

He stares into my face. "Well, smile, asshole." He winces for a moment. "Sorry."

"How can I make you comfortable?" I ask, and regret the question immediately. What a platitude — *comfort!* I realize the man is using the heels of the shoes he's holding to plug the holes in his chest.

"Do you want me to go get Keegan?"

He looks confused. "What for? Where's Thalia?"

I shake my head. "Your wife is dead."

"Bring her to me."

I go to pull the old woman onto the bed. She's lighter than I thought. I have bragged to you all about what a man of the world I am, but I've never seen so much blood. I feel as if a part of my brain the size of a cantaloupe is floating above my own head, checking things out from this safe distance.

The old man from *American Gothic* motions me forward. Suddenly I start to wonder if he recognizes me as his impostor son. The last time we saw each other was in L.A. "I want you to have these," he says, sticking the shoes into my hands.

He's given me his fencing shoes. I'm about to say, *I'm not a dancer,* but instead I say, "The first steps I do will be in your honor."

The old man gives a smile of sorts. "Don't bullshit me about dancing. I watched you move across the floor — you got two left feet." He gives a sudden grimace.

"Should I go get Keegan?" I ask.

He shakes his head. "No. Let me give you something else —"

He doesn't hand me anything. I don't even know what's happening after my face goes flush. My vision starts crumbling into powder. There's this high-pitched whirling. It's like my eardrums are filled with little snails made of glass. Wait a minute. It's like I'm sheldraking.

Another involuntary sheldrake. But not a kind I've ever had before. This isn't my vision, it's someone else's. Wait a minute. I believe the old man is giving me this sheldrake.

We're now standing in a nursery, no longer in Jersey. I look out the window. Manhattan. Downtown looking up. Probably SoHo. Although it's not like the pages of a calendar flick by or anything, I know this is the Reagan era. I hear a baby jabbering, and turn to see a shape in the crib, waving little hands. Doing baby talk.

Suddenly Mr. Lindy dances into the room. He's forty years younger, but his resemblance to Grant Wood's creation is still strong. Lindy is wearing a top hat and tuxedo. Spats! A cane! The works!

"The big Halloween wingding is going to go down at Drug Square," he says.

I translate: The Halloween Parade. Washington Square Park. He's going as Fred Astaire.

Then Ginger Rogers walks in.

Not *the* Ginger Rogers, but Thalia Lindy. She's a young woman too. I know she's going as Ginger because she's wearing "Ginger Wear." That is, she is wearing *the* red dress! I'm sure none

of you Ishmaels have seen Technicolor movies yet. Know that this
dress is more brilliant than my father's Henry James Washington
Square reds. Rogers wore it in a movie called *Bunny Hop*. The first
half of the film was shot in black and white — but not even Ted
Turner had the courage to colorize it, because at the end of the
flick, Fred finally proposes to Ginger in a New York City taxicab.
And they both hop on the cab's roof. And start to dance. Suddenly
the black-and-white roof transforms into yellow. And Ginger's
black dress becomes vermilion. First her bodice, then she turns
and the back of that tight dress — her shoulders, hips, and
haunches — goes aflame too. As the woman completes her spin,
her blond hair twirls into yellow. At this moment back in 1939,
not only did every man in the audience desire Ginger Rogers, but
every woman did too.

And in his SoHo loft, Mr. Lindy looks at his wife and her
dress and cries, "Ginger."

And she smiles and says, "Cigarette me, big boy!" Then lifts
up a bottle of Tanqueray and dabs a bit of gin on her wrists as
perfume. Then her husband takes her by the arm and gives a mock
cry of, "Taxi! Taxi!" And they both dance out of the nursery.

I look around. I'm back in the Lindy bedroom. I look down. The
old man's eyes are rolled up in his head. I'm holding his shoes. I
realize he wanted someone to witness that just before he died he
was thinking of his wife.

Not his nanny.

I have no idea the details of Lindy's jimmy-boo romance with
Keegan — or if he even had one — but I will never reveal his last
sheldrake to that crazy Christian Scientist.

God, I'm a little dizzy, as if I still have a little mental residue. A little sheldrake coming on. Wait. I see Clare. Keegan. Guns drawn. Following the baby cries. They leave through the front door.

"Let's split up," Clare says.

Keegan nods, circles right. Clare goes left. There is nothing behind the Lindy's but backyards. Clare hears stereos and TVs cranking up inside the suburban pagodas. A 7-Eleven is burning across the street — power-line fire. The street itself is full of horse apples. Clare rounds a corner and sees the row of horses themselves tied to a school fence. Beyond, in a snowy schoolyard, stand a circle of nannies.

Clare thinks, *Nannies,* but doesn't recognize any of the girls. And what are they wearing? Then Clare sees, just beyond the first footprints in the snow, all the discarded artillery: .45s. Glocks. Even a Thompson machine gun. The nannies have thrown their weapons down? Clare can't even remember the last time she saw a single unarmed nanny, let alone this.

Then she sees someone familiar — an NBC girl standing at the edge of the group. A nanny with a harelip. I recognize her from Washington Square Park — Katrinka. But wait. My sheldrake says that when Katrinka and Clare bunked together during their training days, the harelip's nickname was Slim. She stands by herself now, absent-mindedly unbelting her cartridges. She's not wearing Flaubert like the others, but I can't even begin to describe her outfit. When I first saw this nanny, she wore a Critique of Pure Reason jumpsuit. Now she is garbed like a psychedelic nun.

"Slim!" Clare calls. "What's happening?"

The harelip turns to Clare. "You! We wondered when you'd show."

"Did you shoot the Lindys?"

Slim gives a smile of sorts. "Not personally." Then she shrugs. "Too bad for them. They wouldn't tell where they dumped the baby."

"How did you know Soda was in danger?" Clare asks.

Slim just says, "The ivory man phoned."

"Who?"

"The guy who pounds the ivory," the harelip says with impatience. "The piano player."

"Caesar?"

Slim laughs. "When I worked for the Lindys his moniker was Augustus."

"You worked for the Lindys?" Clare asks. Surprised.

"Yeah. Five years ago."

"Then you know?"

"About the baby?" Slim laughs. "Sure. We all know about the baby."

Clare looks at the gathered nannies.

"A lot of these girls came out of retirement to be here today." Slim says. Then frowns — a cartridge is caught on a belt loop.

"Stop," Clare says. "I'll fix it."

"Thanks," the harelip says. "You see Dix?"

Clare doesn't answer right away. "Don't you know?"

Slim shakes her head. "Know what?"

"Dix is dead," Clare tells her.

The harelip stops fiddling with her belt. "How?"

"The boss did her."

The harelip stares down at the guns she's discarded: two Glocks and a Ruger double-action six-gun. "Keegan have a good reason?" she asks. But before Clare answers, the harelip just drops her gunbelt. "No big thing. We'll deal with it later."

Slim spins and heads toward the gathering of nannies. "Come on." Then she turns. "Throw down your gun, Clare."

Clare shakes her head. "I can't."

"Too bad," the harelip says, but still leads Clare across the snow and the brown grass, pushing through the assembled nannies. Clare tries to speak to her comrades, but each woman is standing too transfixed. Too gone.

They're doing Cone Heart.

At the center of the circle, the Lindy baby lies naked in the snow, kicking and laughing. Kathleen Keegan kneels at the child's feet.

"Clare!" she calls, not looking up. "I know you're out there!" Her eyes stay transfixed on the baby, her front teeth biting her lower lip — a dental gesture that's weirdly sexual.

"This is so wonderful!" Keegan calls. Then looks up. "Now we know what the Morphic Aberration was."

Clare doesn't get it.

But I do. Keegan means that the Lindy baby was not responsible for making electricity disappear. That child is as innocent as Sigmund Freud or Bob Dylan. The parents are the ones. Don't you think it makes sense that conceiving a child in an elevator at the exact moment Ronald Reagan was shot is Con Ed's "unknown violation" of natural law? First Thalia Lindy gave birth to an eternal baby. Next electricity began vanishing at the bottom of the ocean. Then in New York. Then the rest of the world. Who knows what other acts of nature — everything from sunspots to the L.A. riots — resulted from that union between those two yuppies? Perhaps even the great failure of my life was just one more casualty caused by that fuck between the twenty-second and twenty-first floors so long ago.

Sorry to be crude. I'm sure Kathleen Keegan agrees with what

I've just told you, not that she'd "care a fig." I see the old woman raise her head even higher, tears streaming down her face, her lips gaping in joy. I see all this with my eyes, not through sheldraking — I'm standing here beside Clare, breathless from my running.

"What's happening?" I ask.

"Cone Heart," Clare tells me.

Keegan calls out again. "It's the first time, Clare. This is so, so, so much richer than Animal Magnetism. So much better than Christian Science." Keegan gives a short laugh. "You should have told me it would be like this, Clare." Then she lowers her head. "Come join us. You need Avadhüt now, and the baby needs you."

Clare immediately backs away.

"You're the one to take the baby," Keegan calls.

Other nannies start muttering. "Yeah. Yeah. Take the baby, Clare."

Clare is shaking her head, overcome by the sight of her colleagues — these former Poe girls. Girls with toothache grimaces. Girls with scars. Dented noses. Each now with a misshapen smile. Eyes rolled back. Lips quivering.

Clare grabs my arm. "They're all getting Cone Heart stronger than I ever could!"

Keegan calls, "You're the last one, Clare. Don't be a holdout!" Her eyes are now rolled back into her head like the others. It's as if Keegan has become the old Japanese ice skater pleading to Clare for his glasses. Then I see the baby himself stare up with a look that seems so innocent that the state of innocence is turned inside out. The child begins rattling off a line of baby talk. "Gajaba roo roo roo."

Clare squeezes my arm so hard my hand goes dead.

The baby continues the chatter. "Gajaba roo roo roo, . . ."

Then the baby says, "Caesar."

No! Surely I didn't hear that!

The baby pauses, then I clearly hear him shout joyfully, "Caesar! Caesar! Caesar!"

We can't breathe. Then we can.

Clare grunts, "Come on!"

We're pushing our way out through the nannies as Keegan shouts, "Clare, come back! You know you need Avadhüt! He's your eternal baby now!"

"Am I crazy to run from this?" Clare asks me.

"Hardly," I tell her. I see Slim reaching for Clare's arm, but I block the harelip nanny. She then raises her hand, makes a puppet mouth. "To cheat oneself out of love," the hands says, "is an eternal loss for which there is no reparation."

Clare and I are tearing across the schoolyard toward the street.

"Make for the ferry," Clare says.

As we run, I realize now what the harelip nanny is wearing. It's Danish. But not what you think. Not Hamlet. Nothing from Willie the Shake. That harelip's attire is high Kierkegaard. Not some dingy Fear and Trembling. No. That nanny is covered in nothing less than Kierkegaard's Works of Love.

> "Naturally, I speak of Fred Astaire
> as metaphor."
>
> —Marcelle Clements

9 astaire as metaphor

CLARE AND I wait three hours for the ferry to take us back to Manhattan. Not a word passes between us. I've been hiding Lindy's bloody shoes under my armpit, but Clare grabs them, then begins tapping syncopated rhythms on my suitcase. (When we passed Big Pink I had grabbed Clare's arm, commanding, "Stop! Wait here." Then I ran up the front walk. Where had I left my suitcase? There it was: leaning against the front door. A piano was playing inside. I grabbed my bag . . .)

I now see Clare suddenly smiling at me.

"What?"

"I'm thinking of you standing without a stitch at gunpoint at Radio City," she says, then gives a luxurious stretch and tosses Lindy's shoes into the Hudson. "This feels like the first smile I've had in maybe my entire life."

I'm staring where the shoes hit the water. "That's the exact spot where you threw the gun," I say.

"Yeah." Clare sighs. "I pitched a pair of wingtips here, too." Then she adds, "I'm just feeding the Lady of the Lake."

"But this is a river," I say.

"So sue me," she replies.

We get to the city by dinnertime, but we skip Nell's — neither of us is hungry. Instead, we navigate back to Clare's place in Alphabet City. The nanny nods her head at the front stoop and leads me inside, up to her room. Her apartment is more vivid in person than experiencing it in a sheldrake. I'm compelled to study her bookcases, the spines of her paperbacks all in Japanese. While I examine them, Clare leans over the kitchen sink, splashing her face with water. Water. Wild motion of her elbows. Wild stream of water.

"Are you okay?" I ask.

She looks up from the sink, H_2O streaming down her face. "Yes. I know what I'm doing."

She goes back to her mermaid act. I look away. I'm still not used to her drug thing.

Ten minutes later, Clare leaves the kitchen. "Shall we get undressed?" she asks, kicking off her shoes.

Did I hear right?

It's been so long since romance and electricity flourished that I'm unsure of the correct sequence of events. But I realize that I'm in love with this woman. And love is as dopey as it is religious. And I have something very particular — very dopey — in mind that I want to do to celebrate the return of wattage. Not that Clare has to be undressed to do it. But I remember Clare singing naked last night. "Yes. Undress," I say, smiling.

She starts. "Aren't you going to join me?"

"In a moment."

While Clare slides out of her dress, I open my box and take out something truly marvelous: a small TV and a VCR.

The nanny claps her hands. "Oh, great! The movies!"

"I have a wonderful one to show you."

"One of yours?"

"You'll see," I say, and connect the cables and plugs, pausing every now and then to take her in with my eyes. I have to tell you all that I intend to make love to this woman, and the last thing I want to show her is *The Son from Mars*. No. I will show her a movie that was a cultural high point of the Twentieth Century before the voltage met its Waterloo.

Clare is now sitting on the floor, leaning on a pillow against the foot of the bed.

"Comfortable?" I ask.

She nods and smiles. I smile too and push the Play button. The screen fills with the face of a lion. The animal is bluish in color, and he roars. The title of the movie appears.

"What does that say?" she asks.

"*Royal Wedding*."

"Ah. You're about to induct me into regal love, then?" She gives a laugh. "I don't have any crowns."

Huh?

She opens her mouth for a moment. "On my teeth. I don't have any crowns."

"No. No. No," I say. "This is serious. For the first time in your life, you're about to see Fred Astaire dance."

She raises her hand to her mouth again. "Oh!"

We watch the movie in silence on the floor — me glancing at Clare every now and then. She stares at the screen, her lips open in a slight grin. Is she experiencing Cone Heart? When the flick is over, she says, "Sound makes movies so noisy. Can we watch it as a silent?"

"Sure." I rewind the tape.

I have to tell you that by our third viewing, I am losing interest in Fred. But I say nothing. Instead, I begin running his dances in slow motion.

Before we watch a fourth time, I rewind the tape with the screen running. We watch Fred racing his mad steps backwards.

"Electricity just dances all over the place," Clare says. She has been sitting still for hours, but she is out of breath, as if she's been running. Would I sound like a jerk if I tell you her nipples have been hard for at least three showings? I start the movie yet again and lean over and kiss her. Without much ado, she has me out.

"Wait," I say. "I'll get my Trojan."

"What for? I'm inoculated. Aren't you?"

"Against everything but Lyme disease," I say.

She smiles. "There be no woodticks around here."

I pause. "We still need to be careful. Now that electricity is back, fertility must be as well."

"You know this for a fact."

"I'm guessing."

"I bet you're right."

"I'll get my Trojan."

"No," she says. She's about to say something else but doesn't. I look away, then look back.

"Let's make a baby," she says.

She lets that sink in.

"It's what people do," she says. "Let's make an electric baby. Let's be conscious this is what people are doing and have been doing."

I turn the VCR off. I have never wanted a child. I have never wanted to brush their teeth. Certainly Clare must know neither of us is in any reasonable situation to even muse about having children. But then, maybe I don't know what such a reasonable situation is. Maybe there is no such thing.

"So you want to add another baby to the picture." I laugh. I'm stalling for time.

"Yes. Let's add the baby."

She takes hold of me.

Time's up.

And I can't really stop myself — I don't want to be a father. And I start thinking practically. Forget Twenty Something drugs — I'd just be an old dad — what a drag for the kid . . .

But I've entered her, and we've started our sliding.

"Turn it on," she says.

I don't know what she means at first. She points to the TV. I turn it on and Fred continues dancing. We watch his steps and partake in our joyous friction. And it does seem joyous. Clare is smiling wildly. I look up and see Fred step down the face of a wall. I slide in while Fred steps down. I slide out while Fred steps up. I try to correlate his rhythm with mine. Then Clare reaches out and switches the thing on slow motion. What a girl! This is the first time she's ever seen a VCR, let alone touched a Slow button. Surely Thomas Edison and Mr. Zenith are beaming.

And at this slower pace, Fred and I move perfectly together. I move in. I move out. Fred dances up the wall. Fred dances down.

Clare accepts us both, up or down. And Fred does his dig-step. Clare sees his Irish shoes. Poor shy Fred. Ambitious only to perfection. To serenity. The angels that flew around him were serene and perfect.

And successful.

Wait! I think the word: *successful.* I consider those ten letters as clearly as if I were reading them on the page. Or on a Lit Wear gown or collar.

Success. Speak those two syllables out loud. Is the state of success what it all comes down to in life? I suddenly hear another word, *Rockefeller.* This proper noun beats in my ear. Rockefeller. Rockefeller. Rockefeller. I don't know anything about the man or the nature of his power, but for years his name has been synonymous with success. What about my name: Dylan? Here I am, named after some old folksinger famous long ago. Not exactly a name resounding with success.

And what of your name, Ishmaels? You were each named after a lowly yet elegant pea jacket designed by my father, which was in turn named after the male narrator of a very long, very famous Nineteenth Century fish story, who was in turn named after one of the premier outcasts of the Bible, Ishmael, Son of Abraham, who was forced to wander the Sinai as an outcast. With his mother, of all people! He was such an outcast, that his name meant that very word, *outcast.*

But to hell with outcasts! Ishmaels, I declare that your name means *God hears triumph.* For hundreds of years Americans have tried to make the outcast — the outsider, the rebel — fashionable. Bob Dylan's kid sister once even had an electric hit called "Rock and Roll Nigger," her attempt to give that ugly, ugly N-word ultimate outsider status. But you have *niggered* her one step further by being born Ishmael, the original *nigger.* And by taking this

male name you transcend the political restrictions of your gender. You've grown up beyond the classifications of American
success or failure. You'll never have to worry about some baby
robbing you of your essence. And by that I mean an eternal
baby.

An Avadoot/Avadhüt.

A baby named Soda.

Wait a minute! The word *baby*. I realize that I'm not here in Alphabet City creating an eternal baby with Clare. We're creating an
anthropomorphic child — which is to say that we're just doing
the old-fashioned sex dance that mammals do. It hits me that this
is what I've waited my whole life to do. Create a child, wow! Whatever essence I was robbed of — I now know that I got it back. I
see this clearer than I could on any drug. I know that after this
moment, I'll make movies again. The watts are back, so the cam-
eras can roll. . . .

Hold it! Hold it! How can I have this dialogue with all of
you as I lie coupled with Clare? I should be thinking about babies,
not a resurgence of my Hollywood career. I assume a man in my
position — whether he be an actor or carpenter — should be con-
centrating on the fact that he's attempting to create a life. What did
our fathers think about there inside our mothers? All of a sudden, I
have a dark moment and ask, *What did Mr. American Gothic think
about?* But wait — no! I reject *American Gothic*. I embrace Fred
Astaire. I wear his shoes! I stop sliding and reach down to the floor.
Feel the carpet. Find my shoes — simple white leather loafers. I
grab them.

"What are you doing?" Clare gasps.

"Forget the Lady of the Lake," I say. "Here are my shoes. Now they're yours." I place both shoes beside her shoulders.

We continue our motions. Here it comes. Just before I release myself inside her I wonder, *What did our fathers do at this moment?* My sperm is about to tadpole into Clare. How can I encourage this seed to form a perfect baby? Should I pray?

Suddenly, there is a pounding at the door. What's this? No words. Just pounding. Ferocious raps. We stop. Damn. Our moment is lost. Silence.

Gentler knocking.

Then a baby starts crying.

How can this be? What a forlorn and pitiful sound. *Whah! Whah! Whah!* How could Clare and I have considered making a baby? What a degrading sound — the cursing voice of your own stuff — blood, bone, hormones. What an appalling sound to have haunting you for six months. Let alone for forty years.

Clare suddenly jolts up. "I know those lungs!"

"Huh?"

"I know that baby."

The Lindy child? No. How could Keegan find us?

"I know that crying, I tell you," she says, and starts shaking. "It's Soda."

"Clare, that's ridiculous."

"Keegan knows where I live. She brought us the baby."

How can I argue against this? "We won't answer the door," I say.

But the wailing doesn't stop — the crying just increases. Clare starts for the door.

"Don't!" I say. "We were making a baby. Your baby. My baby. We were not asking for Avadoot or Soda. And Fred Astaire was dancing on the TV."

Clare keeps the chain on the door, but opens it a crack. "Oh God no no no."

I walk over and look. There is nothing in the hallway but a Moses cradle. The stairwell door is cracked open, but I can't see behind it. I feel a presence there. I feel a dozen nannies must be back there, waiting. I'm not sheldraking them — this is just instinct. I peer at the cradle again. I can't see all of what is bundled inside, but two tiny fists raise up. There's all this crying.

I leave the door open a crack, but keep it chained. Then sit on the edge of the bed beside Clare. I guess we'll wait this out. I lean down and turn Fred Astaire on.

"Turn it off," Clare says.

"Why?"

"That was beautiful. This is not."

I turn it off and start getting dressed. Tentatively. In my experience beauty is a successful charm against adversity. I reach for the VCR again, but don't turn it on. I don't because the baby starts talking.

Yes. I mean what I'm saying.

The baby stops crying and begins talking. It's just baby talk at first, then my ears start pounding. Not some deep thudding in my head, but a crisp and brittle beat like a snare drum. And this pounding blocks portions of Avadoot/Soda's patter — and the remaining syllables very clearly form speech. Yes. What I am telling you is true.

The baby talks. And says many more words than a single call of "Caesar."

The baby says, "After forty years, I'm ready to tell my story."

The child pauses, then calls out "Be-ba! Ba-ba! Wee-ba-ba!" Then laughs. Begins another slur of baby talk, then stops and very clearly says, "Just fooling. . . ."

Silence.

Blood in my ears. Clare clutches my hand.

"Ask me what I think about decade after decade after decade," the baby asks.

Clare and I don't say a word.

"The womb," the baby says, enunciating the word clearly. Emphasizing it even. "Yes, I deliberate about the womb. Those wet dark days are still more real than all these dry ones. I'm the only one who can remember what it was like to be drunk on life for nine dark months. Drunk like an Irishman in one of their narrow drinking booths. But then there's birth. And the light. And as the singer says, *He that's not a-busy being born is a-busy dyin'.*"

The baby laughs. "But if Mother was my tavern, what about Dad? If only he could have given birth — Mother would have handed him her small egg and I'd have been born in his lap like a seahorse. You're convinced that it isn't possible for fathers to give birth in this world, but God could change things if he wanted. He is surely that playful. Why else did electricity disappear for all these years?"

The baby is silent for a moment, while I hear something small and fat bouncing on a trampoline: my heart beating.

"I hold God accountable for the blackout," the baby says slyly. "I'm certainly not responsible. The individual moment of my conception didn't sway the nature of reality. Neither did the quantum physics involved between Dad and Mom in an elevator, and the shooting of that old fool Reagan. I tell you that this was of no consequence to natural law. I'm not saying this to avoid responsibility. That's completely foreign to me, because I'm still a baby. Remember? And babies are responsible for nothing."

The child emphasizes the word *nothing* with a roll of the tongue, then laughs. "Who cares what's behind the science of electricity's vanishing act? Scientists are just into blame. They want to blame mammal aggression for the institution of evil. Maternal aggression too. They even want to blame babies for the institution of beauty. Ha! I've heard it said that we babies respond to a beautiful face, and are repelled by those that are ugly. Well, I say line those pretty kissers up and let me respond. Let me evaluate. I tell you that I don't have a clue what beauty is — you all look like big mounds of vanilla to me."

The baby is silent, then grumbles, "You want to know who is responsible for beauty? You want to know who is responsible for the disappearance of electric current? Is the guilty one the same person for each? I know who is, but I'm not telling. Call me Soda. Call me Avadoot. But don't get mad unless you can answer my next question." I see the baby's fists appear above the basket. "The only one I really care about asking: Why am I here?"

The baby's fists begin to shake.

"That's all I ask when I'm drunk. That's all I ask when I'm sober. Hear me shout it from my high chair. From my crib. And when I am quiet and lie sucking at my bottle, be sure that I'm still brooding about it. But no one gives answers. For years I've waited, but none of you has a clue. And all I know is that I did not come to this place on my own accord. Whoever brought me here will have to take me home."

At this, Clare jumps out of the bed and heads to the door.

"Clare. What are you doing?"

She's naked and turns her head over her shoulder. "We have to take this baby home."

She opens the door and leans down to the basket. "And home isn't back in New Jersey!" she says in singsong.

I stay where I am. Here on the bed. This is too much. I turn on the VCR. I'll do something about that baby in a moment, but first let's all watch Fred Astaire.

Ishmaels, let's shoot up his beautiful steps like a drug or dream.

acknowledgments

This novel owes its soul to Conor Lyons's enthusiastic Gaelic edit. Additional thanks to Barbara Epler, Judith Estrine, Monica Vescia, Philip Gwyn-Jones, and Kangaroo Boy.

Electrical consultants include: Andrew Ragan, who first told me that electricity could disappear; David Tomere, who "turned me on" to the work of British scientist Rupert Sheldrake; and Brother Brian Breger, who graciously educated me about Amish technology.

Additional consultants: Bert Schachter (silent movies); Dr. Eric Schneider (Bhisma); Marc Weidenbaum and Mark Malamud (firearms); and Katherine Alpert (patience). Ellen Meltzer and Amy McKinley-Kefauver generously shared their personal observations of babies (additional postnatal thanks to Daria, Noah, Olivia, Jack, and Justine).

Lit Wear was influenced by St. Marks Bookshop (New York) and Dutton's (Brentwood). Fashion accessories provided in an essay by Robert Stone in which he recommends his tailor, Thomas Carlyle.

"Wild Horses" was, of course, written by Keith Richards and Mick Jagger, and appeared on *Sticky Fingers* in 1971.

To save Dylan-speak for the most important thanks: Michael Pietsch is symbolically Bob Johnson, Jerry Wexler, and Daniel Lanois; Paul Harrington and Paul Harrington and Paul Harrington and Paul Harrington and Paul Harrington are Obviously Five Believers; while Sally Wofford-Girand steers our Buick 6 to the Million Dollar Bash.

Finally, I am only familiar with the theoretical principles of beauty because of firsthand experience with my wife, Chloe Wing, who also familiarized me with Sufi terminology, as well as the Coleman Barks translations of Rumi, and Snoot.

A Note on the Type

Portions of this book were set in a digitized version of *Electramor*, a typeface created by Pamela Edison (1868–1943), perhaps the foremost American female typecutter of note as well as a niece of Thomas Edison. As a young woman, Pamela assisted her famous uncle with the development of the Kinescope printing press until the two parted bitterly in 1898 because she had moved into the Waldorf-Astoria Hotel in New York City to be a companion to Croatian inventor Nikola Tesla. A year later, when Tesla was forced to hide out in the Colorado Rockies to elude power company gangsters, she created *Electramor* to commemorate their separation.

This particular typeface belongs to the family of printing types called "modern face" by printers — a term used to mark the change in style of type letters that occurred after the discovery of alternate current in the late Nineteenth Century. *Electramor* avoids the extreme contrast between thick and thin elements that marks earlier typefaces, and attempts to give a feeling of fluidity and longing.

Electramor was digitized by Speedometer Printing, a company founded by Tesla himself (after his return to New York City in 1906) to further his lover's desire to discover a universal typeface. Although she failed to reach her more esoteric goals, Pamela Edison is generally credited as the originator of the "corporate logo." She died with Tesla in an automobile accident near the California-Mexico border.